Whistle Bright Magic

Whistle Bright Magic

A Nutfolk Tale

Barb Bentler Ullman

KATHERINE TEGEN BOOKS
An Imprint of HarperCollinsPublishers

Katherine Tegen Books is an imprint of
HarperCollins Publishers.

Whistle Bright Magic: A Nutfolk Tale
Copyright © 2010 by Barb Bentler Ullman
www.harpercollinschildrens.com

Library of Congress Cataloging-in-Publication Data
Ullman, Barb Bentler.
Whistle Bright magic : a Nutfolk tale / Barb Bentler Ullman. — 1st ed.
p. cm.
Sequel to: The fairies of Nutfolk Wood.
Summary: After her beloved grandmother dies, Zelly and her mother move
to tiny Plunkit, where Zelly searches for her estranged father and helps save the
Nutfolks' home from being destroyed by developers.
ISBN 978-0-06-188286-9
[1. Fairies—Fiction. 2. Single-parent families—Fiction. 3. Fathers—Fiction.]
I. Title.
PZ7.U335Wh 2010   2009014552
[Fic]—dc22   CIP
                                                                                AC

10 11 12 13 14   LP/RRDB   10 9 8 7 6 5 4 3 2 1
❖
First Edition

For two teachers,
Ruth Cruz and Mark Klune,
For two editors,
Julie Lansky and Katherine Tegen,
And for one husband, Jim

Contents

1. Golden, Like Jewelry _⌐ 1

2. Shine upon Our Sister _⌐ 6

3. Three Friends _⌐ 10

4. Fairies? _⌐ 14

5. It Wasn't a Ghost _⌐ 19

6. The Acorns _⌐ 24

7. We Like This Place _⌐ 28

8. Quirky Art Girl _⌐ 32

9. The Gypsy Wagon _⌐ 37

10. Breaking and Entering _⌐ 44

11. A Dismal House _⌐ 50

12. Working Things Out _⌐ 55

13. Vin and Wil Forever _⌐ 60

14. A Dollhouse _⌐ 64

15. Something Strange
about These Woods _⌐ 68

16. The Diary _⌐ 74

17. Everyone Calls Me Whistle _⌐ 81

18. A Strange Hedgerow _⌐ 87

19. Trespassers _⌐ 93

20. That Crazy Feeling _⌐ 100

21. The Mood Catcher _⌐ 107

22. The Shabby Remains
of Nutfolk Wood _⌐ 115

23. Psycho Guy _⌐ 124

24. Feelings in Boxes _⌐ 131

25. Suspecting the Raggedy Man _⌐ 136

26. Trick or Treat _⌐ 141

27. Filling the Gap ⟿ 146

28. The House Rebuilt Itself ⟿ 151

29. Years of Chances ⟿ 157

30. Stubborn Girls ⟿ 162

31. Transformations ⟿ 168

32. Regular Life ⟿ 177

33. Wintertell ⟿ 183

34. Relief ⟿ 191

35. Weird Rendezvous ⟿ 199

36. Shiny and Happy ⟿ 204

37. Honorable ⟿ 208

Conclusion: I'm Good ⟿ 212

Whistle Bright Magic

CHAPTER 1

Golden, Like Jewelry

D ON'T CRY, ZELLY, I kept telling myself. *Don't you cry.*

The trick was to think about other things, like this plain little graveyard overlooking Plunkit. The dead people had a good view of the valley, all right, but by the looks of the patchy grass and worn headstones, it seemed to me that Plunkit Hill Cemetery wasn't getting pampered by nature or man.

And what was with all the plastic bouquets? Tacky, I thought. Although, Grammy used to say that pictures don't have to be pretty to be beautiful. As an artist, I knew this was so. Like ugly dogs and peculiar landscapes, beauty can be terrible. That's what Grammy used to say.

Grr—I was thinking about her again.

In my head a persistent moan was working itself into a sob, and like a geyser under pressure, it wanted *out*. *Don't cry*, a little voice told me, *or something bad will happen*.

At that very moment, an acorn smacked the top of Grammy's casket and rolled off into the grave. *How unusual*, I thought, because, for one, there were no trees above us to drop that lonely acorn, and two, this cemetery was populated by maples, not oaks. And three, the little acorn was golden, like jewelry.

Even stranger was the acorn rising out of the grave all by itself, or so it seemed because I couldn't see the string attached to it. Shimmering like a Christmas ornament in the cloudless sky, the acorn headed right back to the thing that had dropped it in the first place: a toy bird hanging from a floating balloon!

"What are you gawking at?"

I turned to find my great-grandma Cookie in her wheelchair, scowling at me like Mr. Yuk. *Grr.* She was cranky almost all the time, and super old; yet it was her daughter, my funny Grammy Bert, who got the cancer. It seemed as if we were burying the wrong old lady.

"Oh, hi, G.G." I always called her G.G. instead of "Great-Grandma" because it was easier. Plus, the casual address annoyed her, which cracked me up. Before she started in with her usual gripes, I warned her, "I'm in a bad mood."

Her false teeth clicked as she challenged, "*I've* been in a bad mood for a decade."

"I noticed," I said, with audible sass.

Compressing her mouth into a thin, pale line, G.G. shot for revenge. "Willa!" she snapped at my mom. "You ought to remind Hazel Jo of her manners." *Clickety-click* went the loose teeth.

My poor mom had been crying steadily since that morning. After all, Grammy Bert was her mother, and the two of them had been very close.

"Oh, never mind," G.G. grumbled. She was generally more bark than bite.

To change the subject, I cocked my head toward the bird and asked, "What do you think that is?"

"Crows!" G.G. answered, sounding amazingly like one. A bunch of the dark birds rose and scattered near the maples.

"Not the crows," I corrected. "There—the blue bird with the balloon."

"Don't tease." Mom sighed tiredly.

"I'm not teasing. I'm talking about the bird thing, right over there."

Father Bob coughed to cue the service, and G.G. shushed me like a snake about to strike.

Did they all need glasses?

As I scrutinized the silly toy, I decided it was supposed to be a Steller's Jay, only it was missing some parts. The beak and half of the crest were broken off. Spread out in rigid flight, the stiff wings made me think of a balsa-wood glider. But the dumb-looking bird didn't glide anywhere. It just dangled from a gold-colored balloon that had been patched in several places. Curiously, inside a dip on the back of the bird stood a little doll the size of a chess king.

As I watched, a ray of sunshine hit the toy just so, causing a halo to radiate from the doll. The light grew and surrounded the entire contraption, and for a second it shimmered like a sparkler in that bland August sky. And then it was gone.

Rubbing my eyes, I turned back to the ceremony and, there, discovered other eyes looking up.

CHAPTER 2

Shine upon Our Sister

BOY AIMED HIS camera, searching the spot where the toy had been glowing. He must have been about my age, maybe eleven or twelve. The only other person paying attention to the sky was a skinny girl, straining on tiptoes.

"In sure and certain hope . . ." Father Bob droned on.

The girl caught me staring and blinked quizzically.

"Shine upon our sister Roberta Northup," the priest continued, "and be gracious unto her, and give her peace."

"Amen," the crowd recited.

"Amen," I quietly agreed.

As they gravitated into smaller groups, guests were relaxed and jokey now that the ceremony was over. Grammy Bert had lots of friends: old folks and young people and children.

In my head I whispered, *Good-bye, Grammy.* But aloud I snapped, "Let's get out of here," and tugged my mom's hand to get her moving toward the gate.

Mom and I shared the backseat of her uncle's car, where the air was stuffy and hot. I hurriedly rolled down my window, and sat back to study my mother. Even though it is customary for funerals, she shouldn't have worn black. The dark color called attention to her pale, skinny legs and accentuated the bags under her eyes. Grammy Bert would have said she looked like h-e-double toothpicks.

"Now, Zelly, I hope you and your mama will come over tonight," Uncle Andrew urged, adjusting his rearview mirror and polishing a smudge off the chrome with his cuff. We'd driven to the cemetery with my mom's uncle Andrew and aunt Viv in their ancient turquoise Bel Air, an antique car that my great-uncle fussed over as if it were his baby on wheels.

"You can eat and veg out and just do nothing at all," Viv added. She twisted around to talk to my mom. "A respectable turnout, don't you think, honey? I like that Father Bob. He's got a nice way about him. But, Lord, it was hot." She fanned herself for emphasis. "I hope it wasn't too much for the old folks."

"Hey, Aunt Viv," I interrupted, "did you see that bird thingy hooked to the balloon?"

"Where was it?"

"It floated right by us, like maybe ten feet up." Grown-ups could be so clueless.

"I was busy praying." Viv sniffed righteously. "Did you see a bird thingy?" she asked her husband.

"Saw plenty of crows," Uncle Andrew responded. "Whole dang flock of 'em roosting in those maples. Wished I'd had my rifle," he muttered, steering out of the line of parked cars.

"Andrew Northup! To even think about blasting birds at your own sister's funeral—honestly!" Viv glowered at him and then shifted a guilty glance back at my mom, who wasn't listening anyway.

After the U-turn, we drove past the cemetery for a final good-bye, and there, in the shadow of the maple grove, a man stood alone. With a fist to his face and quivering shoulders, he seemed to be crying, but I couldn't see who it was.

Seeing the grown man cry made me want to cry, too. Waves of grief wanted out, but I wouldn't let them. Squeezing my lids shut, I drew a deep breath and, with a mighty effort, managed to halt the flood.

"Let's go!" I demanded, sounding so snotty in my own ears that I embarrassed even myself.

Three Friends

O N A SOFA near the door of Plunkit Books, Mom and I sat receiving condolences. Of course the reception was held there, where Grammy Bert had lived and worked all these years, doing exactly what she wanted to be doing—selling books and bossing people around.

Every summer and holidays, too, Mom and I came to Plunkit for R & R at Grammy's, but this time we'd come to stay. My mother had taken a leave of absence from her teaching job and sublet our apartment in the city. Then we moved into the loft with every intention of calling it home for as long as it took Grammy to get back on her feet after chemo. The only problem was she threw a wrench in this plan by dying.

After an hour of handshakes and hugs, Mom's face was wax-paper white. I cut in line at the buffet table to heap some fruit, cheese, and cobbler onto a plate and then maneuvered my way through the crowd.

"You better eat," I cautioned, setting the plate in Mom's lap. "You know your blood sugar."

"Thanks, Zel. I'll be fine. I'll be fine," she repeated, and made a show of eating the cherry cobbler.

Just then, a woman *click-clack*ed over in stylish high heels. She was a petite, African-American lady in a dark blue suit tailored to her curves. Her hair was sculpted into a tight bun at the nape of her neck, and her earlobes twinkled with diamonds that were companions to her eye-popping ring. From her peep toes on up, she was good-looking, but I'd say more dignified than pretty.

"Willa? It's me, Marla!" she sang, grabbing

Mom's pale hand in a warm squeeze.

Behind Marla was a tall, slender woman. Her beautiful rust-colored hair was gathered in a braid that hung to her waist, and when she moved, she tinkled with an assortment of silver bracelets, necklaces, and earrings.

"It's Debra Henderson now," the tall one announced, displaying her left ring finger as proof.

They were such different women: Marla, the stylish socialite; Debra, the tall, hippie lady; and my mother, a frumpy schoolteacher in black.

"I am so sorry for your loss," Marla said.

"We sure loved your mama," Debra added.

Mom stood up and handed her plate to me. "Thanks, girls," she replied, on the verge of tears again. Then she extended her hand, with her palm facing down.

Marla covered Mom's hand with her dainty, manicured fingers and then waited until Debra's hand covered hers with a long-fingered grasp.

When the three hands were stacked, the women said, "Acorns." They bobbed a funny greeting and then burst into girlish laughter.

Steering me forward, Mom announced, "This is my daughter, Hazel Jo, but we call her Zelly."

"She looks like you," Marla said, studying my face. "But she's a dead ringer for—"

"A MacKenzie," Mom finished.

In that blink of a moment, the three women exchanged a look and then all enthusiastically agreed that I was just like my mother when she was young: brown-haired, brown-eyed, and so cute and clever.

Right. Clever enough to know they were all avoiding the subject of my father.

CHAPTER 4

Fairies?

WHILE THE THREE friends talked a mile a minute, I slipped out the French doors to the deck. Leaning on the rail and mining chocolate chips from a cookie, I contemplated the fact that the Acorns knew more about my dad than I did.

My reserved mother rarely spoke of him, which, for me, hinted at something dreadful, like the guy was a bank robber or an ax murderer or something. But I was pretty sure he was just a loser, if he was still around at all.

I had no pictures of him, no cards or letters, although Mom swore he'd seen me turn three.

She and Grammy claimed that he had "problems," and it was just as well he stayed away. "Problems" referred to his battle with drugs and alcohol, and this was always said together ("drugs *and* alcohol"), which I guess emphasized how really messed up he was. It was significant that my only memory of the man was hazy and distant, a feeling more than anything, a feeling of tension that smelled like ashes and beer.

Sometimes I wondered which would be better: peace and quiet but no father in my life or a dad who wanted me but brought lots of stress. I wished I could have had something in between.

Low on the horizon, the sun was making a color like watermelon smeared into squash. Its rosy light turned the valley golden and the white cows pink. Hushed and hazy, the moist air smelled like cut hay, hanging so heavy in the atmosphere that I could taste the grassy tang on my tongue. Crickets began to sing a drowsy refrain, and the Suquawkal Valley was so pretty in every way that it almost hurt.

The river ran and the fields rambled because people couldn't build in the floodplain; any attempt would have been washed away by the annual high water. I was grateful for the valley and the reliable floods. Inhaling the humid, fragrant air, I closed my eyes and saved the scene with a deliberate mental *click*.

"So, did you see it?"

I jumped. A girl had been sitting on the steps all this time. I realized she was the same dainty girl who'd eyed me in the cemetery.

"See what?" I asked.

"The shimmering balloon," she said, rising to stand.

"Well, it only shimmered when the sun hit it," I pointed out.

"No one else saw it," she continued in her know-it-all tone.

"Of course they did. The grown-ups were only being polite."

"No," she asserted. "Ask anyone and find out for yourself."

"Well, if no one saw it but you and me, then who's crazy, us or them?" I grinned.

Unamused, she answered, "They just don't see as well as we do."

My eyebrows scooched up a notch. "What do you mean 'we'?"

The girl frowned and planted two bony fists on her hips in brat fashion. She had long red hair pulled into a no-nonsense braid, just like Debra.

"Are you related to Debra Henderson?" I asked as the lightbulb went on.

"I'm her daughter, Lupine," she replied.

Smiling to myself, I thought, *Of course she would have a nature name!* "I'm Zelly MacKenzie," I offered.

"I know," she said with annoying superiority.

In the pause that ensued, Lupine stared at me as if I were some kind of bug, until I broke the silence. "Okay. What do you think we saw?"

"You describe something," she coyly suggested, "and then I'll take a turn."

Rolling my eyes at her immature game, I agreed. "All right. There was the dumb-looking blue jay hooked to a golden balloon."

"A blue jay?" she repeated doubtfully. "All I saw was a balloon."

"Well, the bird was hanging from it," I explained. "It was pretty obvious."

Hands still on her hips, she looked thoughtful.

"So, what was it?" I asked again. "Like a circus toy or something?"

Lupine's cheeks went from pink to bright red as she moved in closer. Unmindful of my personal space and with breath that smelled like cookies and milk, she whispered in my ear, "Fairies."

CHAPTER 5

It Wasn't a Ghost

THE FRENCH DOORS banged, and a boy stumbled out. As he raised his hand to greet Lupine with a shy wave, he clumsily knocked a cupcake off his overcrowded plate. It was the other kid who'd been looking up.

"Oh, hi, Frederick," Lupine said, in an uninviting monotone. With the same lack of enthusiasm, she made introductions. "This is Frederick Witherspoon. And Frederick, this is Zelly MacKenzie, Ms. Bertie's granddaughter."

"Hello," he said, stepping squarely on the cupcake he'd dropped. As it squished out from underneath his shoe, the chocolate reminded me of dog poop.

"Our moms used to be best friends in high school," he said. "She was Marla Miller back then, but we're Witherspoons now." He bobbed his head, pleased with the information he'd shared.

Examining Frederick's face, I could see a shadow of the elegant Marla, but her son lacked her sense of style. His thick, dark-rimmed glasses gave his eyes a bulging look, and on his teeth were hefty braces, straining to discipline a sizable overbite. His hair had been shorn close to his head like an overclipped topiary, and with his soft, protruding tummy he was what people used to call "pleasantly plump."

"I'm sorry about your grandma," Frederick said shyly. "She knew I liked weird fact books, and used to call me when good stuff came in. And she was always really funny," he added, showing his wide, metallic grin.

"Yeah," I agreed, "she was really funny."

His appreciation for Grammy, plus his ridiculous smile, made me like him. As often happens when I decide to like someone, his appearance improved ninety-five percent as he morphed from "icky dork boy" into "rumpled pleasant kid" right before my eyes.

Frederick scooched onto a bench and began picking the cake off the bottom of his sneaker. In the meantime, Lupine had skittered to the edge of the steps, unwilling to talk fairies in front of the boy.

Still immersed in cleaning his shoe, Frederick casually said, "I think I got a picture."

"A picture of what?" I asked.

"The fog in the cemetery," he said, flicking more cake out of the tread. Then, giving me all his attention, he asked, "Do you think it was a ghost?"

"A ghost?" I laughed. "It was just a balloon!"

"It was not a balloon," he objected. "It was fog, and it glowed when it came out of the shade."

"Well, it did seem to glow for a second, but it was just the sun reflecting off that goofy toy."

Lupine inched forward, lured by the conflict.

"Did you see it, Lupine?" Frederick asked, hoping for backup.

"It wasn't a ghost," she said, shaking her head.

"But it was sort of shimmery—translucent, I guess you could say."

"It was not," I argued. "It was plain as anything until the sun hit it."

"Well, I got it on my digital camera," Frederick claimed, holding it up as if it were Exhibit A.

Lupine sighed regretfully. "No, you didn't."

"Oh, yes I did!" Frederick countered.

"You just think you did, Frederick. Have you checked the pictures?" Lupine asked.

"No, but I snapped a ton of them really fast until my mom told me to knock it off. Look here." Frederick held out his camera.

We searched a series of photos that appeared on the screen: a tree branch, a cloud, a flock of crows . . . *nothing*.

Bewildered, Frederick snatched the camera back and continued searching the otherwise ordinary images.

"Lupine," I asked, "why were you so sure that Frederick didn't get those pictures?"

Her blush deepened. "I've seen a lot of weird

things around here, and I never get the pictures I want, not digitally and not on film."

"Then what *did* we see?" Frederick persisted.

Lupine's jaw tightened. She wasn't talking.

Turning to Frederick, I tried to keep a straight face. "Fairies," I answered.

As I said the word, something moved near the roof, and although the image was gone in an instant, my brain retained a snapshot. A tiny, boyish figure had stood in the gutter, watching us. No more than four or five inches tall, he had seemed to radiate a mustard-colored light, which went bright blue, and then he was gone.

Feeling unbalanced, I turned back to Frederick and Lupine, who were busy insulting each other.

"Did you say 'fairies'?" Frederick cackled.

"You're just dense," Lupine said.

"Well, you're delusional," he spit back.

As I rechecked the spot where the tiny boy had stood, I thought the word *delusional* seemed pretty accurate.

CHAPTER 6

The Acorns

"So, WHAT'S WITH the Acorns?"

Mom and I settled on opposite ends of the couch in the apartment above Plunkit Books. Exhausted after the funeral and reception, we sat zombielike in the breeze of the fan, picking at leftovers and drinking iced tea. Grammy's apartment was a quirky, comfortable space with mismatched furniture and a huge, deerhorn chandelier presiding overhead. Except for the fan, the big room was quiet.

"Didn't I ever tell you about the Acorns?" Mom asked.

"No."

She sighed. "We were best friends in high school. Different, but compatible. Deb's maiden name was Fetch, an old valley family who homeschooled their kids until Deb put her foot down. She wanted to go to public school, and she got her way." Mom smiled at the memory of her friend's strong will.

"Deb was a smart girl. She may seem all meek and mild, but she is one of the most stubborn, self-directed people I've ever met."

"What about Marla?" I asked.

"In those days, the only other African-Americans in Plunkit were Aunt Viv and a Sudanese kid that the dentist adopted. But what made Marla really different was the money. Her parents got rich during the first computer boom, and back then nobody had that kind of wealth in Plunkit. Plus, Marla sort of flaunted it with all her shopping trips and new clothes. A lot of the kids thought she was a snob, but it was just that Marla knew what she liked and she knew what she didn't like, and she'd tell you all about it."

Mom was grinning again, remembering Marla's smart mouth.

"What about you, Mom? What kind of kid were you?"

"Willa the bookworm, of course. They used to call me Mrs. Science. Pretty corny, huh?"

I smirked. "It sounds about right."

"Yes, your mother was a nerd."

"So you three were the Acorns?" I prompted.

"We started it from that saying 'Mighty oaks from little acorns grow.' I guess we figured we'd all grow up to be something great, plus Deb and Marla were obsessed with my freckle of mystery." Mom held out her elbow so I could see the birthmark shaped like an acorn.

"Mama and I lived up Wicket's Road until my junior year," she continued, her voice softening with the nostalgia. "That's when she redid this loft." Her glance encompassed the apartment, dark now since the sun had set.

"The first two years of high school, the girls

and I would meet at the trailer on Wicket's Road, mostly because Mama was always working, and we'd get the place to ourselves. We made up that dorky handshake, and paid dues, and kept journals . . . all kinds of stuff. It was fun."

"Why didn't we ever visit the Acorns on our vacations?"

Mom's mood hit the brakes. "I closed that chapter," she curtly replied.

I understood that the closed chapter meant *him* and apparently everyone else connected with those years.

"Did the Acorns know my dad?" I asked, trying to sneak in the question before she quit talking.

"They knew him all right," she admitted. "In Plunkit everyone knew everyone else."

"Did they like him?"

Mom's voice went brittle and flat. "Marla used to say he was trouble with a pretty face . . . only I didn't want to believe her."

CHAPTER 7

We Like This Place

ALL MY PLUNKIT days ended in Grammy's office, in the daybed, with the big fan humming a comforting sound and the streetlight keeping me from darkness.

Photos, mostly of me, crowded the walls: my first swim, feeding ducks, skipping stones, helping Grammy in the store. . . . I was a smiling, happy kid. In contrast, I noticed an old picture of my mom scrunched between her parents, Bertie and Mitch. The adults were smiling, but little Willa was not. She must have been eight or nine, unusually pinched and pale for a young girl, more like a worried old lady. Soon after that picture

—◦ 28 ◦—

was taken, her parents split up, and her dad married his "better wife," as Grammy Bert used to say wryly.

"Good night, Zel," Mom said, popping her head in the door. Like her little girl self, she seemed fragile and sad. "Thanks for being so supportive today," she added.

"Sure, Mom." Swallowing a lump of guilt, I remembered being more bratty than supportive.

"You know," she said haltingly, "you don't have to be so brave all the time. It can feel good to have a big cryfest once in a while."

"It doesn't feel good to me," I mumbled. "It feels like something bad will happen."

"The world isn't going to fall apart because Zelly MacKenzie has a good cry." She smiled, but it was pasted on top of concern.

"I'm a thinker, not a crier." It was my standard reply.

"Okay, okay." She sighed, turning to go.

"Hey, Mom, did you see that blue jay thing

floating around the cemetery?"

"'A blue jay thing'?" Pursing her lips, she walked back in and put a firm hand to my forehead, checking for fever. At that particular moment, I thought it best not to mention seeing a little man on the deck.

"This is what comes from eating goodies non-stop," she chided. "I'm surprised you're not barking at the moon with all the junk you ate."

"Yeah. Junk food makes you bark at the moon. Some scientist you are, Mom."

"One of these days I'll regret having raised such a sassy child," she claimed.

"But not today, right?"

"No, not today." Leaning over, she kissed the top of my head.

"What do we do now?" I asked. "What's the plan?"

"I'm on leave through Christmas. Guess you'll be going to Cedar Road School for a few months, and I'll be stuck in the store trying to figure out the mess that Mama left. You okay with that?"

"I'm okay." I shrugged. Actually I welcomed the change. Back at school all my grades, except for art class, were down the drain. It was getting harder to pay attention to facts and figures with so many other things to ponder: pictures, art stuff, and people especially were puzzles to be figured out and understood.

Mom heaved a sigh of frustration and then grumbled, "I thought Mama was leaving the store to Aunt Viv, not me. What was she thinking?"

"That we like this place," I chimed in.

"*You* like this place," Mom corrected. "I've got my job in the city, and I can't take much of this hick town."

CHAPTER 8

Quirky Art Girl

CEDAR ROAD K–8 was like a museum with tall windows, noisy radiators, and chalkboards worn to a useless sheen. The wide wooden halls reflected ninety years of wax and wear and smelled of macaroni, summer paint, and mildew creeping up from the basement.

Even though the school was super old, it was alive with modern artwork. Students' creations brightened the corridors, giving a free and artsy feel to the school. And my fellow sixth graders seemed really nice, not competitive like the kids back at Smarty Pants. Smarty Pants U was the private name that Mom and I gave to the

University International School where my mother was a teacher and where I was a student. It was a brilliant school, everyone said, but for me it was a constant struggle to keep up, except, of course, in art.

Brushing my hair in the girls' bathroom, I looked in the mirror, forced a smile, and decided I looked respectably average. With a straight nose softened by freckles, straight hair courtesy of genetics, and normal black lashes shading normal brown eyes, I figured I was plain enough to go unnoticed.

Still, an inner dread lurked as lunchtime approached. Where was I going to sit? Who would I sit with, and what was the system here?

As I dawdled at the drinking fountain, I forced my anxiety into a mental drawer. I was slurping cold water from the measly trickle when someone hissed in my ear, "I've found something of interest." Startled, I banged my lip on the nozzle. It was that weird Lupine Henderson. *Grr!*

I hated to encourage her, but I was curious. "What'd you find?" I asked, dabbing my lip to see if it was bleeding.

"I'll tell you at lunch," she whispered, and then disappeared.

In the noise and clatter of the large cafeteria, Lupine called dibbs on a table and announced, "We'll sit here." Then she ambushed Frederick Witherspoon and made him sit with us, too.

"I live at your grandma's rental on Wicket's Road," Lupine declared. "Bet you didn't know that." Her little face was smug after surprising me with this information.

"No, I didn't," I admitted, intrigued.

"You'll need to bring permission slips tomorrow if you want to take the bus to my house."

"And why would we want to do that?" Frederick cut in.

"Yeah," I echoed, resenting the domineering Lupine. "What are you, the lunchroom queen?"

Frederick smirked.

"It's about that thing that we saw," she said, nudging me with her sharp elbow and overacting with shifty eyes.

"Lupine, your eyeballs are going to roll out of your head," Frederick warned.

I couldn't help but smile, and decided that these kids might be fun to hang out with after all.

"I'll explain everything tomorrow," she maintained.

Scowling, Frederick took a huge bite of his sandwich, unaware that a blob of mustard was stuck on his cheek, which in no time fell onto his shirt. While Frederick made a big mess with his sandwich, Lupine daintily dissected a tightly rolled tortilla with a fork and a knife and then lined up her grapes on a napkin, eating them at select intervals.

Studying my tablemates, I realized I was aligning myself with questionable personalities. Cedar Road was a small school where all types were tolerated, but everyone had a place. Frederick was the intelligent slob, and Lupine, the know-it-all fusspot. Both kids were a tad odd.

Suddenly, I knew why I was at this table—I was one of them!

"What's so funny?" Lupine asked.

"I think I'm the quirky art girl," I volunteered.

After a moment of grave assessment, they both nodded, and the fact that they didn't question my statement was hilarious in itself.

CHAPTER 9

The Gypsy Wagon

"**N**OT FAR NOW**," Lupine said as the bus turned onto Wicket's Road. "This used to be a pretty drive," she added, "until they clear-cut both sides of the road. Now it's gross." She shook her head in disgust and stared out the window.

It had been a long time since I'd been down this road. Mom and Grammy had shown me the old trailer when I was little, but my memory of the place was nothing like this. With no trees and burn piles stacked bigger than barns, it looked like a bomb had gone off. The undergrowth that remained had been baked by the sun, and now it withered in shadeless ruin.

Coming Soon, a big sign proclaimed, Glen Wood Neighborhood, a haven of luxury homes.

"Ew! It doesn't look like a haven to me," I sneered. "And how can they call it 'Glen Wood' if they didn't leave any trees?"

Lupine shrugged. "Don't ask me. All I know is that I have to pass this disaster every day, and it's depressing."

A logging truck rumbled by, hauling the last of the massive trees harvested from Glen Wood.

"Look at those logs!" Frederick exclaimed, craning his neck to watch them go by. "Bet they're a hundred years old. They don't make wood like that anymore." He sighed.

We stepped off the bus at the hairpin turn onto Voodoo Creek Road and were promptly blasted with a big belch of diesel smoke. The old Blue Bird lumbered away, and we started walking.

The weather was clear and crisp, the three-o'-clock sun mocking us for having wasted the day indoors. In the chill of the September morning, we'd started for school with sweaters and jackets, but now we were peeled down to our T-shirts.

"Man, it got hot," Frederick complained, carelessly dragging his jacket behind him.

"It's nice in the shade," Lupine said sternly. She just had to contradict him.

Glen Wood Neighborhood spread all the way up to the Hendersons' rental, where the devastation finally stopped. There, a distinct wall of vegetation marked the property line, and the natural woods resumed. Under an umbrella of tall evergreens, we were mercifully cool, despite the afternoon sun.

"This is pretty," I said, focusing on the woods ahead. "I'm glad that awful Glen Wood doesn't go any farther."

"Only because your grandma wouldn't sell," Lupine stated. "Ms. Bertie said it was her chance 'to stick it to the man.'"

I smiled. That sounded just like Grammy Bert.

Approaching the little trailer, I was surprised at

how cute it looked after all these years. When she was a child, my mom had dubbed her home "the Gypsy Wagon" for its forest green color and bright red shutters. Bragging, Mom once said that she and Grammy had made a castle out of a junk heap. I'd seen the "before" pictures that proved what an absolute horror the property had been.

Now, the trailer sat like an ornament in a rambling English garden, with rose vines climbing the porch. A carport had been added, supported by stout timbers on rock columns, and the roses climbed there, too.

Through layers of green branches, the sun speckled the pretty scene, and the air was filled with something sweet like tree sap or old blackberries, warm and dripping in the brambles. The beauty of this place floated in the atmosphere like humidity. Closing my eyes, I recorded the feeling and wondered how my mother had ever left.

"My parents are at work right now," Lupine announced. "They both work at Farm Foods." *Of course, the natural foods co-op*, I thought. "But my mom will be home pretty soon," Lupine said.

Lupine unlocked the trailer door and ushered us in. From an open fridge, she called, "We've got vanilla rice milk and some prune bars that are really good!"

Frederick and I looked doubtfully at each other, but my stomach rumbled, sweeping away my prejudice.

"Sounds okay," I replied.

"There's more room in here than I thought," Frederick said, assessing the space.

"It's really cute," I praised.

Sparsely furnished, the trailer was clean and tidy, and everything in it was pale. At the little bay window was a painted white dinette set, situated near a white sofa, which faced a cream-colored woodstove. The only additional color in the room was the soft green and white checkerboard floor, spotlessly clean, like everything else.

"It's simple but really nice," I added.

"It's my mom," Lupine confessed. "She likes things plain. But I got to decorate my bedroom the way I wanted. I'll show you."

Munching the prune bar—which tasted better than it had looked—I followed Lupine to the hallway, where she flung open a door.

The cramped chamber was a shock of orange and violet and yellow, with beaded curtains and sunflower posters.

"I like it!" I approved.

"This is cool," Frederick added, sweeping a hand through the dangling beads at the window.

Lupine flushed and then said, "Oh, I almost forgot! I wanted to show you something I found when we put the new carpet in. Look."

She rummaged through a tiny desk drawer, pulled out a yellowed piece of paper, and handed it to me.

Willa MacKenzie, it read. *Remember Nutfolk Wood*. The penmanship was similar to my mom's handwriting, only wider and loopier. This one phrase filled the page, written over and over again. *Remember Nutfolk Wood*.

"What does it mean?" I asked.

"Well, I don't know," Lupine answered in her bossy way. "I thought you would know!"

I could only shake my head, mystified.

CHAPTER 10

Breaking and Entering

"THERE USED TO be a road here," Lupine explained, "but it's all grown over now." Frederick and I stood in front of the Gypsy Wagon, waiting to follow Lupine on her mysterious trek.

Lupine gestured to a faded FOR SALE sign in the foliage and said, "See that? For, like, twenty years that property's been for sale, only they're asking way too much. Even the Glen Wood guys won't pay the price."

"Who does it belong to?" I asked.

"The Wicket family, I guess," Lupine answered. "That's who the road was named after."

We passed the FOR SALE sign, following a narrow path that, once upon a time, had been a road. After walking in silence for a while, I volunteered, "I was named after Mrs. Wicket."

"Your mother named you Wicket?" Frederick asked, horrified.

"No, she named me Hazel!" I shook my head at what a goof Frederick could be. "She was my mom's babysitter when Mom and Grammy first moved here. So when I was born, Mom named me Hazel because she liked Hazel Wicket so much, and Jo after Jo March in *Little Women*. Only, I wish the old lady was named Lindsey or Laura because nobody names girls Hazel anymore."

"I like unusual names," Frederick declared.

"Same here," Lupine agreed, going against her principle of contradicting everything that Frederick said.

Smiling to myself, I thought, *Frederick and Lupine—of course these two kids would like peculiar names.*

"Ouch!" Frederick exclaimed. He'd gotten snagged by a blackberry stinger and was struggling to free himself.

"I'm bleeding!" he cried, staring angrily at Lupine as if it were her fault.

"Oh, please," she said. "You'd think you were dying. Come on, we're almost there."

The trail widened to reveal a very old house with wisteria clinging to every square inch of it. It reminded me of the enchanted castle covered in rose vines, the one where everyone slept for a hundred years. In fact, I felt sleepy standing there, warm in the afternoon sun, lulled by the buzzing insects and singing birds.

In a sea of wheat-colored grass, the house was surrounded by islands of picturesque outbuildings. Rickety and leaning, the old sheds sagged under the weight of their roofs, where years of decaying leaves had made inches of sod. Now, grass and small trees sprouted from the rooftops like absurd, gaudy hats.

Shading the rickety sheds and the hot, dry grass was an enormous maple tree that had cracked off a sizable limb. The broken bits littered the lawn like old bones, providing hidey-holes for the crickets who chirped as long as we stood quiet and still.

"This is nice," I said in a trance of contentment, although in truth I was aware that *nice* was a lame word for the feel of this place. Even in its lonely neglect, the land, the house, and the air held a beauty that was both peaceful and sad.

Lupine broke into my sense of calm when she ordered, "This way," and swished through the waist-high grass to the back of the house.

"I put a ladder here so I could tie my shoe," she claimed without a hint of humor. A wooden ladder had been propped against the house under an open window. "Come on," Lupine directed, already three rungs up.

Sensible Frederick did not approve. "Isn't this trespassing?" he asked with a frown.

"Yeah," I chimed in. "Wouldn't you call this

breaking and entering?"

"Oh, for goodness' sake," Lupine primly retorted. "We're not breaking, just entering."

Uncertain of Lupine's logic, Frederick and I hesitated.

"I told you," she insisted, "I found something interesting." Lupine was trying to tempt us—and it worked.

"Okay," I finally agreed. "But you're sure that no one checks on this house?"

"No humans, anyway," she said.

"Don't talk like that," Frederick nervously snapped, but she was already through the window and inside the house. Frederick and I followed Lupine, bumbling through the window and into a back bedroom where ghostly sheets covered the furniture.

Speckling the linen were dots of black mildew, which explained the musty smell that hit me like a punch in the nose. Mingling with the must was another bad odor that I could not identify.

"Ew! What's that smell?" Frederick cried with an offended, crinkled nose.

"Mice," Lupine said.

Frowning, Frederick stretched his T-shirt over his nose. "I read about a deadly disease that people get from inhaling the dust of field-mouse poop," he warned through his shirt. "It's called hantavirus."

"Well, I'm not dead yet," Lupine pointed out, "and I've had plenty of exposure." From the bedside table, she lifted a kerosene lamp and carried it out of the room. "This way," she called over her shoulder.

Frederick kept breathing through his cotton neckline, just in case.

CHAPTER 11

A Dismal House

CONTRIBUTING TO THE musty smell of the house was a hint of molding plaster and damp wood, which, along with the potent mouse stink, combined to create a powerful, unhealthy odor. I felt like turtling into my shirt like Frederick was doing.

My eyes adjusted to the dimly lit living room, and I noticed the telltale outline of a missing picture. It must have hung on the wall long enough to keep the rectangle white while the rest of the wall had turned ochre with age. I lowered my gaze to the floor and noticed some dirty footprints.

"Lupine." I tugged on her shirt. "Check out these footprints."

"They're mine," she said, not bothering to look.

"They can't be yours," I argued. "They're gigantic."

She placed her tiny sneaker inside one long print and issued a thoughtful "Hmm, that's funny—they weren't there last time."

"Lupine, you are freaking me out!" Frederick exclaimed, shuffling backward toward the hall.

"Wait," she pleaded. "I just have to show you one thing."

At the far end of the living room, a narrow staircase led to an attic, and Lupine was already climbing the creaky steps.

At the top, we entered a huge, gloomy space crammed with junk. Dirty windows at each end let in a little filtered light, but they were hopelessly clogged by the overgrown vines. The mouse smell up here was not as strong, but the atmosphere was dark and claustrophobic.

Lupine crossed the attic and kneeled next to the far window, producing some matches from her pocket. Expertly, she lit the kerosene lamp, revealing her discovery.

She gestured to a series of unframed paintings and proudly said, "See?"

Propped against the wall was a row of charming and woodsy watercolors—perhaps illustrations for a storybook.

"They're pretty," I said.

"They're not just pretty," Lupine corrected. "Look here." She pointed to a picture with a stump drawn like a fanciful house. "Look at the village green, over by the gazebo. See?"

There was the blue jay that I'd seen at the funeral, only here his beak was whole and his paint job was a fresh cobalt blue.

"Is that the bird?" Lupine asked.

I nodded.

"I don't get it," Frederick muttered. "How is it that I saw a cloud of fog, Lupine saw a balloon, and

Zelly saw this bird thingamajig? It doesn't make sense."

"Yeah," I added. "And how come no one else at the funeral seemed to notice any of it?"

"What I think is"—Lupine chose her words carefully—"it depends on awareness. Or maybe a degree of openness. Zelly, you can see it clearly, and I can see a hazy version, and Frederick sees a hint of it, but no one else in Plunkit seems to have the ability to see it at all—although I'm not sure why."

Before I could digest her theory, something moved outside the window. It was the same apparition of the tiny boy—now perched in the wisteria! His face was pressed against the dirty glass and he was watching us. Or to be more exact, he was watching me, and the gaping look on his face was one of either shock or surprise.

With freckles and sun-bleached hair, the boy reminded me of a miniature Huck Finn. He was dressed in boots and shorts and a long, messy shirt hitched at his hips with a loose, ropelike belt. He was glowing as green as the leaves around him.

I pointed with my eyes and whispered, "Do you guys see that?"

Frederick and Lupine turned toward the window—to behold absolutely nothing. The boy had disappeared in the fleeting second it took them to turn their heads.

"What was it?" Fredrick asked nervously.

Hesitating, I answered, "I think I'm seeing little people."

"Are you teasing me?" Lupine bristled.

"I wish I was."

CHAPTER 12

Working Things Out

BEHIND THE COUNTER at Plunkit Books, Mom was pricing a tall stack of second-hand novels while Aunt Viv sat repairing the bindings.

"I'm here until Christmas," Mom reminded Aunt Viv. "Now's the time to schedule that surgery and get it over with. Then you can come back and manage." She brightly added, "Pick your hours and name your price."

Aunt Viv was so capable, it would be like having Grammy in charge, and then Mom could hurry back to life in the city with a clear conscience.

"You're right about my knee." Aunt Viv sighed.

"It's high time I deal with it. But I have to admit I'm undecided about my future here."

A noisy whoosh of steam announced another latte at the coffee bar. Coffee had always been the smell of Plunkit Books, just as classical music had been its soundtrack. But if Aunt Viv was not inclined to take charge of Grammy's legacy, the future of the bookstore was uncertain.

"Hey, Mom, look at this," I said, filling up the uncomfortable pause. I placed the note from Lupine's room on the counter and waited for her reaction.

"Looks like my handwriting," she said, examining the old piece of paper. "But I don't remember why I wrote it. Where's Norfork Woods?"

"That's not what it says, Mom. You wrote 'Nutfolk Wood.' Does it mean anything to you?"

"No," she said, shaking her head slowly. "It must have been some Acorn thing, but I don't remember what. Does it ring a bell with you, Aunt Viv?"

"Uh-uh." Aunt Viv shook her head no.

"It was in your old bedroom at the Gypsy Wagon," I explained, "and Lupine was curious about what it could mean."

"I don't know what to tell you," Mom said, mildly irritated at her own rotten memory.

Shrugging, I switched subjects. "The trailer looked really cute, and the property was nice . . . except for that awful clear-cut."

"I can't believe the county let them get away with that," Aunt Viv spouted. "And so close to the creek!"

"That old road used to look like something out of a storybook," Mom said quietly. "When I drove up there yesterday to get you, I was sick. I was just sick."

The front door jingled, and Lynn from the café came in, looking for more Edna Ferber. When Mom led her into the stacks, I saw my chance to get a few answers.

"Hey, Aunt Viv, do you feel bad that Grammy didn't leave you this store?"

Her eyebrows arched in surprise. "Not in the least."

"Well, I thought since you and Grammy worked as a team, you might be unhappy about how things turned out."

"To tell you the truth," Aunt Viv confided, "I urged Bertie to leave the bookstore to your mama."

"Why?"

"It's been a fun ride, but I'm tired of the retail grind. And, anyway, Andrew made some good investments over the years. He may look like a redneck"—she grinned—"but he's a smart old boy. We're in good shape financially."

I felt relieved. This detail had bothered me since the lawyer explained Mom's inheritance.

"Zelly . . ." Aunt Viv paused. "Bertie wanted your mother to have the store for another reason."

"So she'd come back to Plunkit?" I speculated.

"Very good," Aunt Viv dryly praised. "That girl has a few things to work out of her system, if you know what I mean. *Closure* is what they're calling it these days."

As Grammy's best friend, Aunt Viv had watched my mom grow up, and I sensed in her a fierce loyalty for the bookish niece she'd acquired through marriage.

Aunt Viv sighed. "Maybe if Willa could forgive your daddy, she could close that broken door and move on. Does that make any sense?"

It made a lot of sense, and I agreed, except for the word *close*. I felt if Mom could just forgive him, maybe she could open that jammed-up door and get out.

CHAPTER 13

Vin and Wil Forever

THE ACORNS DECIDED to get reacquainted by having a girls' night, and we kids were to spend the evening with Mr. Henderson at the Gypsy Wagon.

After our moms dropped us off, Frederick and I found Lupine in the carport pestering her father, who was tinkering under the hood of his truck.

With her girly voice on the edge of whining, Lupine was being her usual demanding self. "So, can we, Dad?"

"Eat whenever you want to," he replied, distracted by the mysteries of his engine.

"And we can roast the hot dogs over a fire?"

"'S okay with me."

"Can I build the fire?"

"It rained last night so I guess I wouldn't worry."

"Can we use the old fire circle in the woods?"

Sighing, Mr. Henderson laid down his screwdriver. "You are a very persistent girl," he said in a droll tone. "Just keep the fire low and drown it when you're done. And Lupine, you're in charge."

This order was dictated with a stern glance at Frederick and me, just in case we may be hooligans waiting to set our clothes on fire or burn down the forest.

Her nose tilted upward. "You hear that?" she said with queenly emphasis. "I'm in charge."

Behind the Gypsy Wagon, we followed Lupine on a trail that wove through a forest so dense, it had its own climate. A million leaves and needles blocked the sun, creating a cool and shady house of trees. From the dim woods, we stepped into startling sunlight, blinking like moles emerging from a tunnel.

"It's so bright, I can hardly see," Frederick complained with a squint that looked distinctly molelike.

"Your eyes will adjust," Lupine sternly informed him.

"It's so pretty," I whispered, gazing at the bright meadow spread out before us. "I think Bambi must live here."

Lupine smiled against her will. It was funny watching her try to be stern all the time.

Next to a picturesque stream was a fire circle surrounded by log rounds that served as chairs. Not far from the ring of stones stood the most noticeable landmark: a tall, pale stump with a water bucket hanging from a notch. As I wandered around the wide perimeter of the stump, I saw something near the base that caught my eye.

I leaned in close and, holding a clump of reeds out of the way, discovered an old valentine carved in the wood. *Vin and Wil forever*, it said.

As I stared at the carving, a bee buzzed near my ear, and somewhere, a blue jay squawked its raucous call. Time seemed to stop, and a sad feeling spread through me. It was so sad, it made me feel heavy and tired. I knew where the weight came from. Vin and Wil were my parents, and they'd carved that heart long ago when they were young and in love. Then all their dreams of romance were ruined by the responsibility of a baby—the baby, of course, was me.

Suddenly, I was uncomfortably warm, aware of how much heat my dark sweatshirt was absorbing. As I tugged the neckline away from my throat, I realized that Frederick and Lupine were standing behind me, watching my reaction.

Lupine opened her mouth to say something, but closed it again. Then she broke my melancholy spell by ordering, "Come on, you guys—help me gather kindling!"

This time I was grateful for bossy Queen Lupine.

CHAPTER 14

A Dollhouse

I SCROUNGED THROUGH THE underbrush searching for kindling and noticed two lines of white pebbles leading into a thicket. Curiosity got the best of me, so I stooped under the branches and crawled into the brush.

Wriggling through the salal bushes, I came upon an unexpected sight: a miniature cabin built out of sticks. It was probably a creation for Lupine's dolls when she was younger.

Still on my hands and knees, I scrunched down farther and fingered the tiny latch on the door. Once I clicked it open, I had to lie on my belly to see the interior. Bundles of plants were hanging from mini rafters above a long table in the center of the room. I reached my hand inside and felt gently around for dolls or accessories, identifying a fireplace, six wooden chairs, and a cupboard with locked drawers. At the back wall, on top of some shelves, was something square. Pinching it between my fingers, I pulled it out into the light.

In the palm of my hand was a tiny book. As I flipped the minute pages, I strained my eyes to decipher the letters and decided a magnifying glass would be helpful. I slipped the book into my pocket, determined to examine it later.

Over my shoulder, I called, "Hey, Lupine, I found your old dollhouse!"

Lupine emerged from the same tunnel through the salal bushes. Standing, she planted her fists on her hips, like she did when she was thinking hard.

Then with cries of "Ouch!" and "Dang it!" Frederick came crashing through the underbrush, sporting a new scrape on his cheek. "What's the big deal?" he grumbled, annoyed.

"It's Lupine's old dollhouse," I said, pointing.

"It's not mine," she flatly stated.

Her face went suddenly pale and she grabbed a tree branch, holding on as if the ground were moving. "It's weird how the house keeps shifting," she slurred.

"What are you talking about?" Frederick demanded. "I don't see any dollhouse, just that light over there." Then, rubbing his forehead, he mumbled, "This place gives me the creeps."

"Are you guys serious?" I asked. "There's a dollhouse right here," I sputtered, stepping forward to bang the roof with my flattened hand. "It's not moving, and it's as plain as the braces on Frederick's teeth!"

"Try the camera," Lupine said.

Frederick focused in the proper direction. "Look, Zel," he confirmed, "nothing."

Indeed, only ferns appeared on the screen, even

though I could clearly see a cabin with my own eyes.

"Maybe another kind of camera would work," Frederick mused. "Like the old plate jobs that require a long exposure."

"Try to touch where you see the light," I suggested.

Stepping forward, Frederick bent to feel for the mini cabin that he could not see. "I found it!" he announced, triumphant for a brief moment, happily thumping the shingles with the palm of his hand. Then his face turned from pleasure to horror as he mumbled, "But I think I'm going to barf."

CHAPTER 15

Something Strange
about These Woods

"SORRY I HURLED." Frederick groaned, mortified over vomiting in mixed company. "There was something about that spot that made me sick. Like, really queasy and weird."

"It's okay," I consoled him, patting his back. "Maybe it was something in the air, you know, like field-mouse poop."

He scowled at the reference.

"Well, I felt strange, too," Lupine admitted. "Dizzy and sort of itchy," she confirmed, rubbing her palms together.

"I must be immune to whatever's bugging you two," I said with a sigh, "because I feel fine."

We were sitting on the logs around the fire pit, watching Lupine place twigs on the small fire she was building. She waited patiently for a sturdier flame before adding the larger sticks.

I pulled the miniature book from my pocket. "Can you guys see this?" I asked, holding it in the palm of my hand.

Frederick tiredly shook his head.

"Your palm is glowing," Lupine observed.

Exasperated with the three versions of reality, I snapped, "It's a book! What's going on here, anyway?"

Lupine's fire burst into a healthy blaze, and she stacked more dry sticks on the top. Then, in her drama queen voice, she said, "There's always been something strange about these woods." Her eyes swept over the meadow. "Ever since we moved here, I've seen sparkles and shadows that can't be explained."

Chuckling, Frederick said, "Yeah, I remember you in first grade. You were always drawing elves and unicorns. You were a weird kid back then, and I think we have to admit that you're even weirder now."

Delighted with his joke, he was still laughing after Lupine jabbed him with her bony elbow.

"Lupine's not the only one seeing strange things," I pointed out. "We all are. I mean, how do we explain what we saw at my grammy's funeral and the dollhouse that wouldn't show up on the camera?"

"We should go back to the attic," Lupine decided. "Those pictures confirmed that we're not delusional."

"I still feel queasy," Frederick whined. "I think I need something to eat."

"Yeah," I said, snickering, "because you lost your lunch."

"By the looks of your gigantic barf, I think you lost your breakfast, too," Lupine added, pinching her nose.

"These are horrible," Frederick declared as he squirted mustard on his third hot dog.

Lupine had produced the thick-skinned tofu dogs, along with condiments and dainty juice boxes, from her backpack.

"If they're so horrible," she glowered, "why do you keep eating them?"

"I'm starving!" he said in defense. "And, anyway, roasting them over the fire makes them taste better."

I nodded. Cooking over an open flame seemed to make food more flavorful, despite the inevitable dirt. In a clean kitchen, ash on the food would be disgusting, but somehow it was no problem here in the woods over a campfire. We ate every dog and drank all the juices, and then practiced the fine art of marshmallow roasting.

"To toast or to burn, that's the question," Frederick said philosophically. He intended to toast them, but they kept bursting into flaming comets of goo. "I think charcoal adds flavor," he lied.

Lupine and I smiled over our schoolmate's blackened failures.

"You realize it's getting too dark to explore," Lupine said with a nod to the sky.

"Yeah, but this was fun," Frederick said.

Shrugging, Lupine couldn't argue.

After a peaceful pause, Frederick quietly said, "I don't think we should tell anyone what we've seen. I mean about the glowing stuff and the cabin and all. People will think we're nuts."

The sun descended below the tree line, and the surrounding woods went black. Embers in the fire pit smoldered like hot lava, and the dim radiance seemed to hold the three of us in a close circle of light.

"You're right about keeping our mouths shut," Lupine agreed in rare accord with Frederick. "We shouldn't discuss it with anyone—not even our parents."

The word *parents* made me think of my own, which stirred in me a wistful feeling that I'd never be able to claim the plural version of that word. Although I understood why things didn't work out between them, I resented "Vin and Wil" for messing up like they did.

When I saw the boy this time, I didn't say anything. He was standing with his hands shoved in his pockets, perched at the highest point on the stump. Glowing with some inner light, his face was clearly illuminated, and when his eyes caught mine, he gave me a decisive scowl.

Funny, it didn't bother me one little bit. Despite the mean look he projected, the feeling that lingered was not hostility or anger—it was loneliness.

Now, why would his scowl make me feel that way?

CHAPTER 16

The Diary

THE *PRIVATE PROPERTY OF Ronald Whistle Bright,* the cover read.

Stay Out! the second page advised. Below that, *A Dreadful Curse upon You, Trespassing Reader!*

So began the tiny book from the cabin of sticks.

I checked the hall and saw Mom's reading light flick off. After her evening with the Acorns, she'd gone to bed in an unusually good mood. It seemed like her old friends brought out a lighter Mom, sillier and younger. And she actually looked prettier!

It occurred to me that she may have been lonesome in the city with just her colleagues from school and her old friend Etta Myers. Occasionally, the industrious Etta would set Mom up on a date, but no one ever seemed to impress her. Those evenings all ended with the same tired phrase "Oh, he wasn't my type." It seemed like no one was her type since my dad.

When I was certain that Mom was down for the count, I opened the minuscule book. Armed with a magnifying glass, I ignored the threat of "a dreadful curse," and began to read.

Auntie Win says that writing in this diary may help rid me of my restlessness. So I'll try, although scratching words don't seem too useful. Mostly what ails me is angst and sorrow that our town is packing up and going north. So go my cousins, and old best friends, and even characters that chafe. So goes all of Nutfolk Wood. And why? Because the humans are coming, and they wreck everything they touch.

Now we were getting somewhere! This is what my mother was attempting to remember with the note she'd scrawled as a kid—*Remember Nutfolk Wood*. That mystical place had faded fast from her memory, and for a time, she had known it was fading.

In days of old, Nutfolk Wood did thrive. The weather had been our friend for many a season, and although old Hazel had passed, we were confident that her good daughter would come tend the garden. Trade in the foothills was high, instances of illness were low, and babies were a blessing. But then the current shifted.

It was the winter of cold and ice when my parents met their end, stalled in a surge and crushed on the highway by a careless hum truck. This tragedy, compounded by the cold and dismal weather, set folks to thinking in a glum tide. What if the daughter never came? The forty acres could be taken by another, perhaps by crashers and builders. It would happen fast, as it always did, and our town would be in a storm with folks surging like refugees.

Scouts began to observe patterns, watching the spread of crashers from the river to the foothills. After several seasons, the results were undeniable. The hum mess was spreading directly east from the river and following the wide gash of highway. They were coming all right, and with no like-minded benefactor, Nutfolk Wood was doomed.

At least that's what everyone said when the subject came up, and it came up often.

The vexing thing was that nothing bad actually happened after the death of my parents. No crashers growled at the glen and no

pavers came to spew rock, but the general
state of mind was so negative and resigned
that folks began to leave. Just a dribble here
and there as this family left to meet that fam-
ily. But as the seasons passed, the population
dwindled, and the poor town lost its hearti-
ness and its health.

Now townsfolk say, "Why stay in this
crack-blasted ghost town when there be better
glens to put down roots?"

But I say, why scatter? This here's our
town.

I felt a lump in my throat for the author's pre-
dicament, caught up in a tide of events he couldn't
control—first losing his parents, now losing his
town.

I flipped hurriedly to the last page and read on.

Auntie convinced the town council that our
wood should award the gold acorn to the
momby of an Honorable called Willa.

So they were the ones who dropped the acorn at Grammy's funeral! And "an Honorable called Willa"? Was that my mother? What made her so important? I couldn't help but think of the birthmark on Mom's elbow: an acorn so perfect, you would have sworn it had been drawn there.

Madam Healer made a big noise and got that old toot Calm Stilts from maintenance and Grampy, of course, to drag out the jay.

At first light, I checked the window and scanned the green. There sat the old bird with his head crunched from tragedy, lashed to the patched balloon. With its fill of hot air, it rose like a fat harvest moon, looking grand and golden in the sun.

So ironic to fly the jay again to honor a crack-blasted hum, when its last trip was to deliver my parents to their death, and for that I can thank the heedlessness of men.

Well, the writer did not like humans. He had a grudge, big time, after his parents were killed. Plus, with all the development going on, the end was near for his Nutfolk Wood. He was right. Someone was going to buy that property and slap up a bunch of houses. His little town was doomed, just like he said.

"Sorry, Mr. Bright," I whispered out loud.

"Return my book!" A voice demanded from somewhere inside my room.

CHAPTER 17

Everyone Calls Me Whistle

STANDING RIGIDLY AT the foot of my bed, hands thrust in his pockets, was the same small boy I'd seen before, now with an angry spark in his eye.

"Didn't you read the warning?" he demanded.

"I read it," I admitted, "but I didn't believe it."

He paused. "Yeah, well, there ain't no curse," he finally said with a shrug. "But you shouldn't have read my pages—'twas pesky rude!"

"I'm sorry," I said in earnest, and then I realized I was still holding his diary. "Here." I placed the book on the bed for him to retrieve, but the snoop in me wished I'd read faster.

"Would you turn off that crack-blasted machine?" he asked with a fierce motion toward the desk.

The only machine was the computer on standby. "You mean this?" I asked, pointing my thumb toward the modem.

"Obviously. Doesn't that thing make your skin crawl?"

"No, but I'll turn it off," I assured him, hurrying across the room.

"And the lamp," he added.

I switched that off, too, although I could still see him with the light from the street.

"Are you Ronald Whistle Bright?" I asked as I flopped back onto the bed, making him bounce a little.

"Who wants to know?" he said, sounding all tough.

"I'm Zelly MacKenzie, Willa's daughter." I hoped my mother's name would mean something to him.

"Must be you take after your momby," he

muttered, "because humans are generally dumb as logs."

Refusing to be drawn into an argument, I asked, "Why do you say I take after my mom?"

"She could see," he replied, "and so can you."

"But she can't see you people anymore, and, in fact, she doesn't remember a thing about Nutfolk Wood."

"Most hums are too busy up here," he said with a finger to his head, "so they can't see the glen through the trees."

"That doesn't explain why she can't remember," I pointed out.

"Perhaps a healer fogged her dreams," he offered. And then, he curled his lips into a secretive smile and said, "It's what you might call a security measure."

"Well, how come I can see you?"

"Don't ask me, because I don't understand you in the least," he snapped. "Guess you are a freak of hum nature."

"That's mean!" I charged. "It's not my fault that

I can see you, and I apologized for taking your diary. You don't have to be insulting."

Cocking his head and squinting, the boy seemed to be assessing me. "'Tis unusual in these times for a human to see us," he said, staring at me with unflinching green eyes. "You are a rare read," he added, more to himself than to me.

Under his gaze, I squirmed but found it hard to pull away, and something compelled me to confess in more detail.

"I found the diary in that cabin," I blurted, "but I didn't realize it was personal. I looked at a few pages—at the beginning and the end—but I certainly didn't read any private stuff, not about who you like or anything."

With the savvy of a human boy, he understood I was referring to girls and scoffed, "There's no one to like unless you count old toots and aunties."

He snickered, and I giggled, and for a brief moment we found ourselves laughing together.

"How old are you?" I asked, sensing a lull in his grouchiness.

"Fourteen springs," he answered.

"I wouldn't have guessed. You look small for your age," I began, realizing too late that I didn't mean to say *small*, which he obviously was, but I had meant to say *young*.

"What I mean to say is that you seem— Oh, never mind." I stopped myself from babbling, figuring that, either way, calling him young or small could be interpreted as an affront. Finally, I just started laughing at myself.

Smirking, he assured me, "I'm average among my friends and small only by your measure. And I might add that, by Nutfolk scale, you are hugely enormous."

"Thanks," I replied, miffed at being described as enormous.

A long pause ticked between us. Finally, he said, "Well, I've got my book, but you mind your tide, Zelly MacKenzie," and he wagged his finger at me as though he were scolding a cat.

I realized that, like G.G., he was more bark than bite, acting gruff to keep me distant. After all, his poor parents had been killed by "dumb hums," and now his hometown was at our mercy. Plus, there was no one his own age to hang out with! Of course he would have a chip on his shoulder.

"I'm sorry about your parents," I said. "And I'm sorry about the trees being cut and humans moving in everywhere. And I'm really sorry your friends have moved away. It makes me feel bad."

Giving me a stilted nod, the air around him began to shiver and buzz, and his body grew more translucent. He was almost gone when his voice crackled from the haze: "Everyone calls me Whistle. . . ."

CHAPTER 18

A Strange Hedgerow

"I T WASN'T A dream!" I said again.

Frederick and Lupine and I sat around the burned-out fire circle on this warm Sunday morning, pondering my latest news flash. After I relayed the story of my encounter with Whistle Bright and described the contents of his diary, Frederick and Lupine were noticeably quiet.

"I'm telling you the truth," I repeated. "I met him and I talked to him, and his name is Ronald Whistle Bright, but everyone calls him Whistle."

"Zelly, I've seen some odd things around here over the years, but nothing quite so . . . detailed," Lupine finally said. "It sounds really interesting and all, but it sounds like a dream."

"Well, it wasn't a dream," I objected. "At least, I don't think it was." Logic was eroding my resolve.

"Lupine, you saw the balloon and the cabin. And there's something about these woods—can you feel it?"

Lupine shifted her eyes. "Like we're being watched."

"Are you two trying to freak me out?" Frederick croaked.

"I think we are being watched," I agreed. "That boy doesn't have anything better to do because his friends have all moved away."

"Well, I want proof," Frederick snapped. "How do I know that you two aren't making up stories?" He glared at Lupine and added, "Some people do have very active imaginations."

"You mean intelligent people?" Lupine quipped.

In an effort to stop their bickering, I suggested, "Why don't we try to find that little town? We can look at the paintings again, and then we'll know what landscape to search for."

"Okay," Frederick agreed. "That's logical."

Smirking, I thought to myself that searching for a fairy town in the woods was the most illogical thing I'd done in my life.

"Um, my parents don't exactly approve of us trespassing up there," Lupine confessed. "I sort of got in trouble when they figured it out."

"So what are we supposed to do now?" I griped.

"Take the back trail," Lupine said, undaunted.

Lupine's back trail was an exercise in bushwhacking. Before long, the meager path disappeared, leaving us to make our way through woods that hid a minefield of holes and dips and foot-catching roots.

"This is why I never go this way," Lupine called from the lead, untangling her braid from some prickles.

At the top of a knoll, we discovered that we

could see the roof of the homestead and began to descend toward smoother terrain. Surprisingly, the forest cleared and Lupine stopped short. I banged into her, and then Frederick bumped into me. "Ouch!" we all said, reminding me of the Three Stooges.

Lupine, who'd caused the collision, was standing dramatically still. "Look at that," she said, tilting her head like a curious terrier.

The only thing worth her remark was a patch of salal bushes in a clearing ahead.

"There's something unnatural about the way they're growing," Lupine muttered. "They're too tall, and the patch is too square."

To prove it, she darted ahead and ran around the salal bushes.

"They're growing in a big rectangle," she said, panting, as she rounded the corner. "Let's get a bird's-eye view." Immediately, she began climbing the nearest Doug fir until she was ten feet up.

"You guys need to come up here!" she called.

Frederick rolled his eyes but took the challenge, and I followed him. We had to squeeze through a tangle of branches but finally got high enough to see the lay of the land.

I was stunned by the sight below. It was not a patch of salal bushes, but a hedgerow encircling a beautiful garden. The rows of flourishing fall crops were straight and weeded—acorn squash, orange pumpkins, lacy carrottops, purple cabbages, and some kind of bean. Many rows were bare, resting under layers of leafy mulch. Put to bed for the winter, Grammy would have said.

"Who did all this?" I asked in amazement.

"I have no idea," Lupine answered, equally baffled. "I didn't know this garden was here."

Frederick aimed his camera and noted the image on the screen. "We're all seeing the same thing, right?"

I nodded. "It's like the Secret Garden," I whispered, "only after the kids fixed it up."

"It's perfect," Lupine agreed, "and in just the

right spot to get lots of sunlight but still remain hidden."

"Look at how neat the rows are," I observed, "and there are, like, zero weeds."

"Someone's taking care of it," Frederick reasoned.

Immediately I thought of Whistle's diary. *Although old Hazel had passed, we were confident that her good daughter would come tend the garden.*

"It could be a neighbor using the land without permission," Frederick suggested.

"People around here have property," Lupine said doubtfully. "It doesn't make sense for someone to sneak into the woods to raise vegetables."

My eyes scanned the hedge and followed the line of foliage around all four sides, and I realized that there was something very odd indeed about that garden.

"Did you guys notice that there's no way in?"

CHAPTER 19

Trespassers

AFTER WALKING AROUND the hedgerow a second time, we confirmed that there was no door or gate, and, in fact, there wasn't even a gap big enough to put your arm through.

"There's no denying how weird this is," I said gravely. "Maybe now you'll believe that I really talked to that kid."

Lupine nodded thoughtfully. "I believe you, Zelly."

"Well, I'll believe it when I see leprechauns," Frederick muttered as we reached the top of the knoll.

Autumn had transformed the old house, coloring

the wisteria a cinnamon shade and the leaves on the maple a bright yellow. In the yard, the over-grown shrubs had gone fiery red, looking like flames arising from the yellow grass. High above, a clear sun and sapphire sky amped up the colors in everything.

"Wow," I said, clicking the picture in my brain for safekeeping.

Following Lupine, we descended to the front yard and began to cross to the back when our leader raised her arm to halt.

"Tire tracks," she whispered, examining the ground. A vehicle had driven through, pressing two tracks into the lawn.

"We should get out of here," Frederick said.

"Let's just peek around back and make sure no one is breaking in," Lupine proposed.

"You mean like criminals?" Frederick looked stricken by this awful possibility.

"Come on, let's be good neighbors," she cajoled.

Once again, Lupine's nerve surprised me. She

was so skinny and pale that I didn't expect her to be brave—or was she just being foolish?

"Let's take a look," I decided.

Swallowing a dry gulp, Frederick shook his head in silent disapproval, but he was outvoted.

From the back of the house, we could see that the tracks continued from the yard and into the field, where apple trees dotted the wide-open pasture. In the farthest corner, parked under a tree, was a junky black pickup truck.

"What right does that person have to be here?" I challenged. "I mean, unless he's a Wicket, he's trespassing, too!"

Lupine nodded. "True, but—"

At that moment, something growled in the tall grass, and to my horror, the biggest dog I'd ever seen stepped out of the field. Approaching us stealthily, like a wolf on the prowl, was a Great Dane the size of a pony. He curled his lip into a snarl, as his rumbling growl shifted from neutral to warning.

Frederick and I turned to Lupine, seeking

instruction. Our fearless leader said one word: "Run!"

Lupine was fast, with me a close second, but Frederick lagged behind. Just as I was cursing his dumpy slowness, my foot caught a mole hole, and I slammed down onto the ground. The smell of earth and grass was strong in my nose as I gritted my teeth and tried to get back up.

Frederick was suddenly above me, grabbing my arm and jerking me off the ground. "Run," he ordered. "I'll distract him."

The dog loped around the corner of the house, growling like he meant business. I'd already reached the trees when I checked back to witness Frederick waving his arms.

"Over here, ya dumb dog!" he cried. Throwing himself on the ground, Frederick rolled into a ball like a potato bug. He'd distracted him all right!

The monster barked from deep in his throat as he walked stiff-legged toward Frederick. I could see the fur on the back of the animal rise, and with every step, he growled louder. Tightening the grip on his knees, Frederick braced for the end.

I couldn't leave him to be mauled, so I started limping back to the scene. All of a sudden, Lupine sprinted ahead with a big stick in her hand.

"Back off!" she yelled, waving her weapon like a baseball bat.

Amazingly, the beast changed his mind, his body language altering from predator to pet. He sat amiably next to Frederick, his tongue sprawled out in a bored pant.

Astonished that Lupine's order had been so quickly obeyed, I hobbled forward and held out my nervous fingers. "Good doggie, nice doggie," I coaxed with high-pitched, phony friendliness.

He wagged his tail and rewarded me with a slobbery lick to my palm.

"Frederick," I said softly, "you can get up."

Opening one eye, he seemed pleased and surprised to discover he still had all his body parts. Wary of the gigantic canine, Frederick moved cautiously and sat up cross-legged, just as the dog apologized by licking one side of his face and depositing drool all over his glasses.

"Good doggie," I said again, scratching him under his chin. "He doesn't seem mean now," I observed.

"I think we startled him," Frederick theorized, "and he reacted."

"You were really brave," Lupine said with a dawning expression of respect on her face. "I didn't know you had it in you."

"Yeah," I agreed, "you were like some kind of hero." I stared at him as if seeing him for the first time. I realized the immensity of what Frederick had done, putting himself in harm's way to save me. "Wow, Frederick, that was the bravest thing I ever saw."

Unwilling to bask in our praise, Frederick changed the subject. "We better get out of here before the dog's owner comes looking for him. Can you walk?"

I nodded, and then realized I'd forgotten about my ankle, which now was beginning to throb. As I limped into the woods, supported by Frederick and Lupine on either side, I couldn't get over the admirable traits of my new friends. Lupine's exterior was girly and prim, but she had been ready to club that big dog with a stick. And Frederick, the chubby coward, had been willing to sacrifice life and limb . . . *for me.*

A shrill whistle cut the air. "Eddie!" a deep voice bellowed.

As I jumped to flatten myself behind a tree, I glimpsed the owner jogging toward his dog. I took a mental snapshot of a tall man with a black jacket, baseball cap, messy hair, a beard, and a scowl. He was just as scary as his dog.

The monstrous Great Dane, Eddie, now sat perfectly content, with Ronald Whistle Bright hanging onto his neck and whispering something in his ear.

CHAPTER 20

That Crazy Feeling

AFTER SCHOOL ON Friday, we took the bus to Frederick's house in the Highlands, where Lupine and I had been invited to try out his hot tub.

Rumbling up the other side of the valley, the bus came to a stop at an electronic gate, where the bus driver had to lean out the window to type in a code.

"She hates this run," Frederick said, snickering, "because she has to open the window and get all cold and wet."

The black metal gates opened smoothly, and we proceeded down a lane of large and beautiful homes where everything seemed orderly, tasteful, and quiet. Turning backward, I watched the gates close and lock.

"This is my stop!" Frederick called.

We shuffled out the door with a crowd of kids. "Just up here," Frederick directed as we approached a stately home.

It seemed like acres of roof covered the brick and cedar chalet, with ample room for cars, boats, an RV, and a nanny if they wanted one. I entered a grand hall and was struck by how elegant everything was. Lupine, on the other hand, clearly disapproved of the excess.

"Frederick, you guys are making a huge impact on the environment," she scolded. "Why do you need such a big house for the three of you?"

"I don't know." Frederick shrugged. "Why don't you ask my parents?" he said slyly.

Marla had bustled into the hall to greet us, along with Frederick's dad, who I learned was named Stewart.

I could tell by Lupine's hands-on-hips body language that she wanted to lecture the Witherspoons on thrift and the environment, but her code of courtesy prevented it. Besides, Marla was warm and friendly, and Frederick's dad had ordered pizza.

The Witherspoons' spa was sunken into a back deck overlooking a vast yard and greenbelt. Despite the chilly twilight, we sat immersed in the steaming water, stewing like chickens in a pot.

When Frederick turned off the noisy Jacuzzi, the deck became quiet, and as darkness settled on the landscape, some twinkly patio lights blinked on.

Now and then, scraps of autumn leaves drifted down from the tall trees, dawdling as if they were enjoying the trip. When a sudden gust of wind whipped through, the dead leaves scurried across the lawn in mini twisters, and the bare branches waved their bony fingers.

"Ooh, it feels like Halloween." Lupine shuddered.

"How's the trick-or-treating around here?" I asked.

"My neighborhood is the best," Frederick replied, not bragging, just confident. "People compete with decorations and sound effects and give out full-sized candy bars!" His face was shiny with moisture as he looked up at the stars, recalling past candy triumphs. "It's really great." He sighed.

"We usually go to a potluck at my nana's," Lupine volunteered. "My parents don't approve of all the candy."

"Why does that not surprise me?" Frederick replied, heavy on the sarcasm.

"We are pretty different, aren't we?" I mused. "I mean, look at where we live: Frederick here in this big house, and Lupine in a little trailer in the woods, and me with my mom in an apartment above a bookstore."

"But we all get along okay," Frederick added like a diplomat.

Lupine refused to get sentimental. She just said, "I guess."

"So, does your dad live around here?" Frederick asked nonchalantly.

"Frederick!" Lupine pitched him a withering glare. "We weren't going to ask, remember?" she enunciated between gritted teeth.

"I was just wondering." Frederick's voice cracked defensively. "I mean, lots of kids live with one parent," he sputtered.

Glancing from Lupine to Frederick, I realized that they'd been discussing me.

"It's okay," I assured Lupine. "The truth is, I don't know where he is. He had, you know, alcohol problems and left when I was small."

"Oh." They both nodded.

"Was that who carved the Vin and Wil heart?" Lupine asked.

"That's right," I muttered.

"I always wondered," Lupine confessed. "I used to make up romantic stuff about that heart."

"Well, desertion isn't exactly romantic," I pointed out. I suddenly felt overly warm, so I sprang up to sit on the edge of the hot tub. Even though I was self-conscious about being in my bathing suit, I had to get some air.

Why'd I have to get stuck with a loser dad who never bothered to visit or even send a birthday card? It was pitiful to know so little about him. But then it came to me—perhaps knowing the whole truth would be even worse!

"It's just as well he stays away," I mumbled, surprised to find myself repeating Mom and Grammy's phrase—only I sounded ten times more bitter. And the same dread that pursued me at the funeral was threatening now—that crazy feeling that accompanied grief. I turned from Frederick to Lupine and felt almost sick to my stomach as they stared at me, shocked by what I had revealed—until I realized they were staring at something behind me!

"It's him," Frederick breathed. "It's the boy you talked to, Zelly."

Turning my head, I saw Whistle peering out from behind the railing, no bigger than a toothbrush and glowing like a firefly.

Despite the melting heat of the spa, Lupine shivered and wriggled with excitement. "I see him, too!" she hissed.

Embarrassed by being found out, Whistle's cheeks flushed red, and this time he disappeared with noisy feedback and static. Even after he vanished, the low buzz lingered, and the air continued to glow in the spot where he'd stood.

"Okay, I saw a leprechaun," Frederick conceded.

CHAPTER 21

The Mood Catcher

"SOMETHING WEIRD IS going on," Lupine declared on the phone.

"What's up?" I asked.

"A real estate agent, that's what."

To annoy her inner drama queen, I yawned and said, "So?"

"So? A car from Hart's Realty is parked in front of my house right now, and that obnoxious Jimi Hart is getting out. He's with another guy. Ew, he's got a really big butt, and the back of his jacket says GWD."

"What does that mean?" I asked.

"Glen Wood Development," Lupine grimly

informed me. "Maybe they've decided to buy."

"Oh no," I said weakly.

"'Oh no' is right," she agreed.

That night, the boy materialized with a mild hum and stood on the edge of my desk.

"Hi," I said. "You could knock, you know."

"Knock what?" he asked, surveying my room.

"Never mind. I'm glad you dropped in. I couldn't sleep."

"Neither could I," he admitted.

"Lupine said there were people snooping around Hazel's old house—a real estate agent and some guy with a big butt from Glen Wood Development."

"What's a big butt?" Whistle asked, straying from the subject.

I pointed to my rear.

"Oh." He nodded and smiled just a little. "And Mr. Glen Wood is the forest wrecker?"

"Yes. I hate to say it, but I think they're

considering buying that property. Your town, if they come in with the big equipment— Well, you saw what they did down the road."

"Took every tree and mucked up the stream," he said in disgust.

I nodded glumly as a snapshot of the devastated Glen Wood rose in my mind. I shuddered to think of what may be in store for the lonesome homestead with its rambling fields and natural dignity.

"If only someone nice would buy that property!" I wished out loud.

"Why don't you buy it?" Whistle suggested. "Then a sympathetic human would be in control."

For a second I thought he was joking, but then I realized I was the only human he knew.

"I'm a child," I said, pointing out the obvious. "Children can't buy land."

"Children can't do much, can we?" was his sour response.

"You're able to do lots of stuff," I argued. "You can turn invisible and zip around like magic."

"We don't zip," he objected. "We surge."

"Well, I wish I could do it."

"We're not so different, you and I," he reflected. "That's what I was thinking the night I caught your mood clear."

"What do you mean 'caught my mood'?" I asked, suddenly uncomfortable.

"That night you were in the hot pot, I caught the feelings that live in your mind."

"You were reading my mind while I was sitting in the Jacuzzi?"

"Not exactly. It's more like looking at a picture of your truth, that's all."

"Oh, that's all," I mocked.

"We share similar family disappointments," he continued, "and we use similar strategies, like fanning the angst."

"Fanning the what?" I grinned.

"You know, carrying the stone on your back."

I started giggling at our cultural miscommunication. "You mean having a chip on your shoulder?"

"That's it!" he cried. "It's a strategy, you see? Anger confuses the sadness."

He'd read me correctly: calm on the outside but hurting inside, attempting to deflect with bursts of snotty anger. It didn't fool him one bit.

"I guess we all have issues," I agreed.

"Issues." He nodded.

"Before, you were just a blur to Frederick and Lupine. How come we all saw you that night?"

"The senzall went thin when I caught your mood."

"What's senzall?"

"Sort of an energy byproduct. It acts like a screen, and when I was distracted with sympathy, the screen went thin."

Appalled at the idea of him feeling sorry for me, I decided to double-check. "Do you mean sympathy like pity?"

"Like understanding," he corrected.

"So while you were snooping in my brain, you let down your guard?"

"Exactly!"

"Can all your people catch moods like you?"

"No!" he scoffed, surprised at my assumption. "We all read the auras, which give us a general impression, like what frowns and smiles do for you. But the mood catcher gets all the details and cannot be deceived. The knowledge is instant and true." Shifting his gaze, his eyes locked into mine, and I had a feeling he was reading my mood as he spoke.

"We are often physicians," he went on, "and healers of the mind. Or else we go odd and become lunatics, burdened by overload."

"Which are you?" I asked, growing uneasy with the boy's intensity.

"Lunatic, of course," he claimed.

"No, you're not," I flipped back. "You're smart—and perceptive."

He hoisted one appraising eyebrow and replied, "As are you. And I think we might help each other."

"How do you mean?" I asked.

"I want to stay in my hometown," he confided. "And you want to stay in your book house. Would you concur with this truth?"

"I'd definitely concur," I said, smiling at his quaint way of putting things. "But how can we help each other?"

"When I have a strategy, you'll be the first to know." He was pleased with his own mysteriousness.

"Whistle, did you do something to that dog at the homestead? I saw you for just a second, the day we got chased."

His smile broadened at the memory. "Oh, him. Nervous fellow, that Eddie. I calmed him with some mild senzall and told him a little joke was all. When he got to laughing, he lost interest in you three."

"You told him a joke?" I asked, heavily skeptical.

"Well, I'm not going to repeat it!" he said, aghast. "It wasn't exactly polite, if you track my current."

His expression changed, and I was sure he was reading me again when he said, "You are quite untypical. Most humans glow like dirt or, at best, with fleeting virtue, but there's something unique in the way you shine that has puzzled me from the start."

"Maybe because I'm creative," I suggested.

He smiled, but his reply sounded doubtful. "Maybe."

CHAPTER 22

The Shabby Remains
of Nutfolk Wood

"**D**O YOU THINK he'll show?" Frederick asked, tossing another pebble in the sodden ashes of the fire circle. The bleak Saturday was cold and gray, with rain on the horizon.

"He doesn't like humans," I admitted. "But he's curious, and he's lonesome. I think he'll show."

Craning my neck, I scanned the meadow and checked the leaden sky. Dark clouds were looming in the west, and cold gusts kept charging over the field, battering the grass.

"It's after noon," Lupine grumbled, consulting her watch and huddling her knees in close. "I thought you said he'd be here at noon," she complained.

A faint crackle preceded a glow, and the three of us watched as Whistle materialized on an empty log seat.

"I see him!" Lupine gasped, fairly trembling with excitement. "But he's all blurry."

Whistle hopped down from the log and touched Lupine's ankle. She jolted like she'd been Tasered. "I see him perfectly!" she exclaimed.

Frederick got tapped in the same manner, but maintained his composure. Only his wide-open eyes betrayed his astonishment.

"How's it going?" Frederick asked, making a good attempt at being calm.

"It all goes with a certain amount of anxiety," Whistle carefully replied. "You understand that my people don't normally associate with your people, so you must swear never to speak of what you see this day."

"We swear!" The three of us bobbed our heads in eager cooperation.

"Swear upon your honor, and know that I can

read your deceit as plain as a bad book."

There was something threatening in his tone—he didn't say "or else," but we all sensed it. Standing taller, we recited, "We swear upon our honor!" Frederick held up his hand in a Boy Scout salute.

As he faded like a hologram, Whistle directed, "Right, then. Follow the markers!" and he vanished.

"Look, there's a light!" I shouted, and we were off. The markers were leaves glowing like Christmas lights. As we dashed through the woods in search of the phosphorescent leaves, we were swept up in the thrill of the hunt.

Soon, we'd passed the Secret Garden and were crossing Voodoo Creek on an old foot bridge, where the remnants of a trail twisted and led us uphill. Here, the woods were silent and dark, the huge trees towering to unseen heights. In the gloom, the thick bark looked lavender and the forest floor black. Chilly and damp, the air smelled distinctly earthy, like mushrooms and mulch.

Another glowing leaf signaled a turn, and we squeezed through a wall of huckleberry bushes. Under low cedars and over fallen snags, we finally stepped into an improbable clearing. On a nearby branch, Whistle balanced gracefully, and without fanfare, he announced, "We're here."

Panting, I could hardly believe my eyes. With a stump like a little apartment building and rows of tiny cabins gathered around a miniature public park, I beheld the shabby remains of Nutfolk Wood.

At one end of town stood a bench-sized building made of small gray rocks, speckled with damp, green moss. A sign on the bell tower proclaimed Town Hub. Next door was the Postal Hub, a delicate structure built from what must once have been white pebbles, discolored now to sickly green by the moss.

The largest complex was topped with a sagging sign that read Nutfolk Wood Trade Center, with various subcategories like GROCER, CLOTHIER, and COBBLER, all part of the shingled mini mall.

The residential homes curved around the town, climbing up a small hill to one side. They were similar in style and size to the cabin at Lupine's, built with sticks and rock chimneys and cedar shake roofs, but they appeared mostly empty. The shutters on the tiny windows and doors were closed and latched.

A tree stump had been converted into a house, and with numerous windows and interesting balconies, it was a handsome example of their architecture. But again, the shutters were closed and the arched front door was boarded with a LEAVE BE sign, hastily written and pounded crooked onto the jamb.

The settlement presented a sad picture of neglect. On the porches were piles of leaves and litter that no one bothered to sweep. Yards were overgrown, chimneys were crumbling, windows were broken, and the enemy moss was threatening to envelope the town.

A movement in the overgrown park drew my eyes to an old Nutfolk man chipping on a wood-block with a hammer and chisel. On the ground next to him lay the detached wooden Steller's Jay.

Suddenly annoyed, the old elf spotted Whistle and demanded, "What're these dumb hums doing here?"

"I brought 'em," Whistle stammered. "They're the hums—the humans I told you about, Grampy. You know, the ones who can see."

Squinting, the little grandpa faced us. He was the chess king I'd seen on the back of the bird!

"So you perceive this here village?" he inquired.

Obediently the three of us nodded. "Yes, sir."

"I'll be cracked," the old guy mumbled, and then he spit. "Don't s'pose it matters anyhow, since this here town ain't long for the liv'n'."

Glancing toward the wooden Steller's Jay, I asked, "Why did you drop that acorn at my grandmother's funeral?"

"That one be momby to the Honorable," he said, "so we owed her the nod and, of course, a minor good deed."

My face assumed what must have been a "dumb hum" expression, so he tried again.

"To show the weight of respect and the tie to the Nutfolk," the tiny man elaborated with obvious impatience.

"How was my grammy tied to the Nutfolk?" I asked.

"She be momby to the Honorable," he repeated, "and there's not many left these days—the folk could count 'em on one hand."

"What makes a person Honorable?"

"Aid or protection of the folk and their property," he recited like a schoolboy. "Valor in particular, and strength of character as well."

"So my mother aided Nutfolk?" I was astounded at this new information.

"Indeed. When she was a child."

"What did she do?"

"Tried to fight off an auto ride." He chuckled. "Some log-headed hum thought he'd buzz through the glen, and your momby decked him. Righteous, she was, and tough for a skinny thing."

I was enjoying thinking of my mom in this new light when I remembered the acorn mark on her arm, her freckle of mystery.

"Would she be marked in some way?" I asked.

"You might find a mark if you was looking," he agreed. "Most likely the crest of the family or town—by crack, you're a talkable hum, ain't ya?" he accused.

Under his breath, Whistle urged, "Grampy, don't keep calling them hums."

"Right!" Grampy's head moved up and down. "Right you are. Forgot my manners," he boomed. "Just never conversed with, er, humanity."

"Why can't more humans see you?" I persisted.

Grampy considered this carefully. "It's like when you drive your auto rides and you're zipping fast along the lane. You cannot focus on the little things; they come and go and leave no impression. Only it's your brain that's driving fast, with the next thought overlapping the last thought and most a heap o' trash anyhow. It's like that."

I had to smile at Grampy's vague and puzzling explanation. To hear him tell it, most humans were shallow creatures living hurried, pointless lives. In defense of humanity, I exclaimed, "We're not all dumb logs, you know!"

"No, I didn't know that," Grampy confessed, displaying genuine interest in this unlikely possibility.

CHAPTER 23

Psycho Guy

"WE SHOULD GO," Lupine warned, interrupting the fascinating Grampy. "I think a storm is coming."

I surveyed the treetops and watched clouds piling up like dark pillows. As a chilling gust whipped around me, I shuddered. Just then, a flash of lightning preceded a crack of thunder so violent that I jumped and cringed at the same time.

"Let's go!" Frederick shouted over the wind.

"Good-bye, Grampy!" I called as we turned to run. "Good-bye, Whistle! And thank you!"

We squeezed through the huckleberries and then rushed over the bad trail as fat bullets of rain splattered all the way down to the forest floor. That's when my foot caught a root and yanked the ankle I'd already twisted.

"Slow down!" I yelled to Frederick as pain seared up my leg. "I twisted that darn ankle again!"

"Lupine!" Frederick called ahead. "Let's go to the homestead for shelter."

Arriving at the back of the empty house, we scurried up the ladder and climbed through the window. With another zap of lightning, thunder even louder than before rattled the glass, and then a torrent of water fell from the sky, as if a giant had turned a hose on high.

"Man, what a downpour!" Frederick shouted as Lupine closed the window.

"It won't last long," she predicted with her usual confidence. "Let's take another look at those paintings."

Once we were in the attic, Lupine lit the kerosene lamp so we could find our way in the gloom. Then, after setting down the light, she placed all the paintings against the wall.

I sat on a stool to give my ankle a rest, then examined the images of old Nutfolk Wood while Frederick busied himself taking a series of photos of each painting.

"Look, here's the secret garden," I pointed out, picking up a stiff watercolor. "There were a lot more rows of vegetables back then and no salal bushes at all."

"Here's the stump house," Lupine added, examining another picture. "The paint was brighter in those days," she said. "Look at the trim."

"It used to be a much smaller town," Frederick observed. "But it was in a lot better shape."

The old watercolors depicted just a few homes surrounding the park—no town hub or post office or trade center. Between then and now, Nutfolk Wood must have expanded like crazy and then dribbled off as its people lost faith and started to flee.

Frederick tilted his head and got a peculiar look

on his face. "Did you hear something?" he asked.

"Like a car engine?" Calm but alert, Lupine quickly extinguished the lamp.

We padded downstairs and headed to the back bedroom, where Lupine opened the window and emitted a strangled yelp. Stepping up on the ladder, right outside the open window, was the sopping-wet dog owner, smiling.

"Well, well, well," he said in a low voice, "if it isn't my mysterious trespassers."

Stunned, we stood there gaping. Then, with the dog owner still on the step, Lupine pushed the ladder as hard as she could. "To the front door!" she screeched.

Not waiting to watch him crash, we scurried to the door. Lupine flipped the bolt and swung it wide, but the screen door was locked as well, and she wasted precious seconds fumbling with the latch. Finally, we were free, racing up the path with speed fueled by panic.

This time I was the slowpoke, trying to keep up

with my stupid sprained ankle. *Almost to the Secret Garden*, I thought. Just then, I misplaced my foot ever so slightly, and my wimpy ankle betrayed me with a sharp sting of pain. I was going down!

"Hey, kid," the man said, standing over me. "You okay?"

My heart lurched in my chest and my mouth dried up as he reached out a smudged and dirty hand. I wasn't sure if he intended to help me up or grab me, and I was surprised to find myself slapping the hand soundly. "Leave me alone!" I shouted.

"Look, I didn't mean to scare you," he assured me. "But I want you kids to quit trespassing in that house."

Still sitting on the forest floor, I felt vulnerable, but angry. "You're the trespasser, you psycho! You're the one sneaking around with your ratty truck and your mean dog. We're just nosy kids, but you're a creepy adult."

Taken aback by my fierce speech, he stood

quietly, looming over me like a shadow. He withdrew his outstretched hand and then shook his head like he was amused.

It was hard to get a fix on his features with evening settling in. His beard and hair seemed longer, his eyes indistinct in the shadow of the baseball cap. I felt relief in knowing that he couldn't see me any better in this dim light. With my hood up, I doubt that he could tell if I was a boy or a girl.

"Look, I just don't want anything happening to that house," he said calmly, "and I know you kids are playing with matches in there."

"We weren't playing!" I shouted. "We only lit a lamp to explore with. And we were really, really careful. Unlike you—driving on the grass and letting your crazy dog attack people. You're the menace," I declared, pleased with my word choice.

Now the man chuckled. "The best defense is offense," he said to himself. "You're a funny kid," and as he said it he laughed, but then his face lit with a new expression.

"What's your name?" he asked, his tone more intense.

Except for my pounding heart, the forest was quiet, until a faint hum escalated into a buzz, making the hair on my arms stand up. Relief flooded through me as a smirking Whistle Bright materialized on the man's shoulder. Glowing warmly in the purple dusk, Whistle pointed a casual finger toward me.

A static charge cracked, and I found myself up on my feet and racing into the woods, pushed along by a force like an itchy wind.

Soon I was joined by Frederick and Lupine, who had appeared from behind trees. Lupine took my hand and pulled me along, and in case the man pursued us, Frederick bravely followed last.

CHAPTER 24

Feelings in Boxes

THAT NIGHT, FREDERICK e-mailed the pictures he'd shot in the attic, and I studied each one closely. In view of Whistle's claim that humans rarely saw the Nutfolk, it seemed bizarre that these images had been recorded. Yet here was painting after painting depicting every detail of the glen. Who was this artist?

Opening a picture to full size, I checked the signature. *Rachel Meeker*, it said. Meeker? The name hit me like a freight train—Meeker was my father's name.

At the kitchen table, Mom was adding columns of numbers. After a long day in the bookstore, her hair was messy and her blouse had a coffee stain the size of her hand. Although she looked tired, there was a sparkle in her eye.

"Every day is better than the last," she said gleefully. "Sales are really good!"

"Who is Rachel Meeker?" I asked, getting right to the point.

Startled, she looked up. "Your grandmother on your father's side," she soberly answered. "She died long before you were born."

"What was she like?"

"All I know was that she was a good artist, like your dad—and like you. How'd you hear about Rachel?"

"Over at Lupine's," I answered vaguely. Mom's secrets were beginning to annoy me, and I snapped, "How come we don't have any pictures of my dad around?"

"I threw them out."

"Did it occur to you that maybe someday I'd be a little curious?" I asked in my snippiest tone.

Unrepentant, Mom replied, "I had to move on. My job was to be a good mother to you, and I couldn't do that if I kept grieving over him."

"So you threw everything out—including him?"

"I was young, Zel, and I did the best that I could." There was something steely in her tone and in her gaze. I wondered if she was acting tough or if Willa the bookworm was stronger than I'd imagined.

"Aren't you even curious about him?" I asked.

"Not anymore."

"A little worried?"

She sighed. "I put all my worry and hope in a box, and I closed the lid."

Funny. She put her feelings in boxes, and I organized mine in drawers.

"Maybe you didn't search because you were afraid of what you'd find," I said, trying to place blame.

"Maybe you are exactly right."

Mom exhaled like she'd decided something.

"Look, Zel, he was in bad shape when he left. Really sick and unpredictable."

Rubbing her forehead like the memory gave her a migraine, she said, "Near the end, we were fighting all the time. You were little, but you understood the tone, and when we raised our voices, you'd cry 'til you were sick."

Way, way back in my memory was a sense of anxiety accompanied by a sound, and the sound was me, crying. There were yelling matches and fights, incomprehensible in their adult concerns, but they all featured one word that I understood—*Zelly*.

For a moment I held the memory, but then it was gone, slipping through my fingers like water.

"After I told him to leave," Mom continued, "he disappeared completely. For all I know, he could be living on the streets somewhere—he was that messed up. I'm so sorry, Zelly, but that's the truth."

It was easy to imagine the chaos. A young

couple struggling with their new little baby. Fights, drunkenness, disappointment, heartbreak. If Mom hadn't taken a stand, I could be living it now.

Back then, my infant self did the only thing she knew how to do with her feelings—she cried. And then something really bad did happen. He left, and he did not return.

CHAPTER 25

Suspecting the Raggedy Man

SO MY DAD could be on the streets somewhere like a homeless guy. Turning restlessly in bed, I flattened my pillow with a punch. I closed my eyes and tried to recall the face of the raggedy man on the ladder: black hair under his baseball cap, dark eyes in the shadow of the brim, a crooked nose, the scar on his lip, the unshaven jaw—like someone who'd known hard times.

I could picture the hand reaching out to me, long-fingered and discolored with splotches. Was it paint?

That was it—he had paint on his hands! His

mother was an artist, and he was an artist—just like me.

Tall and slender, his build was the same as the guy in the graveyard, the one who seemed to be crying. A strange feeling came over me, and the more I reflected, the more my stomach flip-flopped with an emotion I could not name.

Crossing the room, I turned on the computer and searched for Vincent Meeker, certain that I'd find something on the man or his art. Disappointed, I came up with nothing at all. I returned to bed, wondering how much of what I was feeling was intuition and how much was imagination. One thing I knew for sure: I just had to go back to that house and find him, to learn the truth.

At school, Frederick, Lupine, and I met at the usual table at lunch. Originally we'd planned to discuss tonight's Halloween agenda, but when I told them about my theory, our plans began to shift.

"So you think that psycho guy could be your

dad?" Frederick managed to express both doubt and dread in his tone.

"I think it's possible. It seems likely that he would have heard about Grammy Bert's funeral, and then maybe he returned to the old neighborhood. Plus psycho guy and the man in the maple grove had a similar look about them."

In a low voice, Lupine suggested, "How about instead of going to Frederick's tonight, you guys come to my house and we'll go confront him?"

"That idea stinks!" Frederick protested. "First, it means we won't score any candy, and second, we'll be creeping around on Halloween night with that monster dog and crazy man in the woods."

"You make it sound so bad." Lupine sniffed.

"It is so bad!" Frederick practically shouted.

"Well, let's not go unless we all agree," I said. "I mean, we can always wait, even though it is really hard for me to sit and wonder about my long-lost father."

Frederick groaned, shaking his head. "I tell you, I don't like it, I don't like it, *I just don't like it!*"

Mr. and Mrs. Henderson prepared to leave for their traditional Halloween potluck. "Nana's only three minutes away," Mrs. Henderson repeated as she put on her coat. "You just call if you're scared, and Dad and I will zip home."

Nana lived up the hill on Voodoo Creek Road, and all of the Henderson clan would be there. But Lupine had convinced her parents that we wanted to stay at the trailer, to tell scary stories and hand out apples to trick-or-treaters. Frederick rolled his eyes, plainly disgusted with the notion of an apple being anyone's idea of a Halloween treat.

Once her parents had gone, Lupine assured Frederick, "Nobody ever comes down here anyway. It's too creepy on Wicket's Road."

"I know!" Frederick cried. "That's my whole point."

Lupine ignored his grumpy outburst and

instead handed us each a flashlight from under the kitchen sink. With businesslike authority, she asked, "Frederick, did you bring your phone?"

"I did," he said, "but the service up here isn't very reliable."

With an evil grin, Lupine announced, "I have my pepper spray!" and she held up a can with her finger on the trigger, demonstrating how ready and eager she was to inflict pain. Pocketing her weapon, she opened the front door and happily sang, "Let's go!"

CHAPTER 26

Trick or Treat

A BLUSTERY WIND KEPT pushing the clouds in front of the moon. One minute it was bright enough to make shadows, and the next minute the world was snuffed into darkness.

We turned on our flashlights and began walking along the old road. Since the truck had gone through and flattened the grass, the trail was easy to follow.

"He's up there," Lupine said in her low voice. "I smell wood smoke."

"That's because everyone around here has wood-stoves," Frederick said, pointing out the obvious. The air was fragrant with the smoke of seasoned wood and the tangy smell of unpicked apples molding on the trees.

Shuddering, I had to admit to myself that the man may be just a creepy stranger. Then I shuddered again when I thought he could be my real dad, only unchanged and still an addict.

"Burr," I muttered, gathering my jacket close. "It's cold out."

What I hardly dared to hope was that he *was* my real dad and done with all his bad habits. That's why I didn't tell Mom. If the man was Vincent Meeker and he was still a mess, she didn't need to know. But if there was a crumb of hope, maybe we could open that box together.

The weird yip of a coyote ricocheted over the field, and Frederick jumped. "Did you hear that?" he whispered.

"It's only a coyote," Lupine said, unimpressed.

"They've been known to attack children," he lectured.

"Just boys," she lied.

"There's a light in the house," I interrupted.

We studied the building ahead.

A glow from inside flooded the yard with a warm yellow light, and we could see that things looked different—the grass had been mowed and the suffocating vines had been ripped off the exterior and piled to one side in a gigantic heap. The windows seemed shinier; the porch had been scrubbed. It appeared that psycho guy had done some cleaning.

A ribbon of smoke drifted from the chimney and vanished into the limbs of the maple. As we moved closer, we heard music: strings and piano in bittersweet accord, wavering from tinny speakers inside. There was something heartbreaking in that music, something infinitely sad.

Summoning my courage to climb the porch steps, I whispered, "I'll do the talking."

Obscured by the screen, I could see him sitting on the couch in the living room, playfully directing the symphony with a fork. A plate of dinner and a bottle of water sat on the coffee table. Lit by kerosene lamps, the room was bathed in a golden light that flattered the man playing maestro; he seemed more boyish than menacing.

Suddenly, Whistle was sitting on the window-sill, grinning. I decided that he must be spying on us most of the time because he always seemed to know where we were.

Before I chickened out, I took a deep breath and rapped assertively on the door.

Startled out of his wits, the man jumped and kicked the coffee table, which knocked something else. From an unseen stand, a picture swooped gently downward. It was a painting on stretched canvas, a work in progress depicting the moon in a black sky with leaves swirling in a frenzied breeze. The scene got filed away in my head as a moody autumn vision, beautiful and somehow dangerous.

A frantic clatter of dog's nails on wood preceded the appearance of the monstrous Eddie, who pressed his nose against the window and barked as if he wanted to rip my head off.

"Down, Ed!" the man commanded. "Sit!"

Amazingly, Ed sat.

When the door cracked open, I sang out, "Trick or treat!"

Flustered, he replied, "I—I don't have any candy!"

"Then I get a trick," I curtly responded. "You have to tell me your name."

When he opened the door a notch wider, I could see that we shared the same dark hair, the same long lashes, and the same straight nose—except his was altered with a crick and a bump, as if it had been broken.

Peering out, he said, "I know why you're here."

"What's your name?" I asked again.

He held out his hand to shake and answered, "Vincent Meeker. Hazel Jo, I presume?"

My mouth went sticky and dry as I answered, "You presume right."

CHAPTER 27

Filling the Gap

"WE'LL JUST TALK from the porch," I said.

"You're careful and that's smart," he agreed.

Whistle interrupted the exchange by piping in, "I read his character true, and there is no danger here."

Although Mr. Meeker was oblivious to big-mouth Whistle, I shot the boy a glare, willing him to be quiet so I could concentrate.

"These are my friends Frederick and Lupine," I continued.

He nodded respectfully, waiting for me to take the lead.

"So, what are you doing here?" I finally asked.

"I got permission from the owner's daughter," he quickly replied. "Kathryn Wicket Pommeroy— she said I could hang around for a while, so long as I cleaned up the place. I suppose I wanted to work some things out."

"Did you come back here for Grammy Bert's funeral?"

"I did." He nodded. "That's what got me back, and then I couldn't leave."

"Did you stand by the maple trees and cry that day?"

This surprised him. "I didn't think anyone saw," he confessed, a little sheepish.

"Yeah, well, I did." Then, as tactfully as I could, I asked, "Do you still have, you know, *problems*?"

"I quit all that stuff," he said in earnest. "I've been clean and sober for almost five years."

Pausing, I formed the question I had come to ask, although I dreaded asking it. Involuntarily, my voice went high and soft, like a younger child's. "If you've been healthy for five years, why didn't you come and see me?" Tears glazed over my eyes, but I held myself tight.

"I didn't have the nerve," he confessed, glancing down at his feet. "I was afraid I'd be interrupting your happy life."

"Well, I'm here, aren't I?" I snapped, hoping that if I sounded irritable, then I might actually be irritable and the lump in my throat would subside.

Quietly he said, "Yes, you're here. You're a brave kid."

"So why didn't you visit my mom?"

"I didn't want to bother her," he mumbled, brushing crumbs off his jeans. He seemed to be stalling. "Did she, well, find someone else?" Glancing down through his lashes, he flushed a telltale pink. "I mean, it's good if she did, because I can't imagine she wouldn't. . . ."

"There's no other guy, if that's what you're talking about."

"Oh." He nodded, absorbing the news, and then

his mouth formed a smile that reminded me of my own. With the same lanky frame that I saw in the mirror, this man explained my long feet and fingers. His existence also explained my passion for art and my obsession with pictures, and I realized that something was filling up in my heart, as if all this time there'd been a gap that didn't exactly hurt, but it wanted to be filled and had never been quite right!

"Everyone calls me Zelly," I said as the warm feeling spread.

"And everyone calls me Vin."

Still smiling, he stared at me and I could feel my cheeks getting hot. Mercifully, he turned to Frederick and asked, "Are you Marla's kid?"

Frederick nodded.

To Lupine he said, "And with that hair, you must be a Fetch."

"Fetch was my mother's maiden name," Lupine primly retorted.

"I'm glad to meet you both."

An awkward pause descended, and a wintry gust fanned my hot cheeks. Like a spotlight, the moon chose that moment to shine.

"What now?" I asked him.

"Good question," he replied, but that was no answer.

I looked up into the man's eyes. I could tell he was thinking—thinking hard.

"Can people start over?" he asked out of the blue, almost pleading.

I didn't know what to say.

CHAPTER 28

The House Rebuilt Itself

AFUNNY THING HAPPENED to Vincent Meeker that night. I know because Whistle wrote it all down and left miniature pages of testimony pinned to my pillow in the morning. I grabbed my trusty magnifying glass and began to read Whistle's account.

After Zelly and her friends left, the work of the night began. Trickentreat was over, and the poppy snuffed his lamp and crawled into his sleeping sack to ponder the brave and stubborn daughter he'd just encountered.

I liked that part, Whistle calling me brave and stubborn.

Hours passed, and finally, when I could read the color of sleep wafting around the man, a band of elders appeared. Grampy was there, and Auntie Win, and the carpenter Calm Stilts, and the last of the garden farmers—five crabby old gentlemen, plus their wives.

No one under thirty springs could join this band of tricksters, because no one under thirty springs was left in Nutfolk Wood. But good surging requires mental dexterity more than physical fitness, so the oldsters were up to the task.

The job was fun, concocted as a quick fix to remind the human of his childhood days, spent with the old lady Hazel. It had been a sweet home back then, and therein lay my plan. I wondered if a fresh vision of this house might restore some sense to the grown man of just how much it needed saving.

I told Grampy my notion, and he liked the lark of it, so he urged the others to follow. It was a quiet procedure, with no banging or sawing of physical work, but only the faint hum of surging, over and over, until the air grew hazy with the dry fog of senzall. So thick was the mist that the man could not have roused out of slumber if he'd wanted to, while through the night and into the morning the house rebuilt itself.

All the refuse from inside was levitated out and heaped onto a mountainous pile of rubbish below the house. The plentiful mouse habitats were sent to the field, much to the surprise of the mice themselves and amidst their squeaky objections.

Moisture, rot, and all things smelly were surged elsewhere, mostly to field and wood, as plaster walls collected into smooth surfaces, and glass in the window panes reflowed until they were solid. Floors were sanded with particulate, and the dust was sent in a stream to the pile.

Grampy elected me to lift paint from the darkened town market. The oldsters had argued earlier about color, and after much discourse and debate, it was finally decided. Tan to the parlor, cinnamon to the hall, yellow to the kitchen, and green in the bath. And in the bedroom, a pretty shade of lavender. The paint was surged onto walls without dripping a drop.

For furniture, we shined up some pretty pieces, reweaving upholstery and surging the mildew away. A farmer's wife took an interest in the kitchen and made sure the stove was spotless, as well as the sink and the old gas cold box. The oil lamps sparkled and the wood floors gleamed, and when Grampy restoked the fire in the stove, the house was a picture of home.

By the time the sun was bright in the window, we'd finished, pleased and proud. Surely this man or some other would value the house as a home and not merely as junk in the path of a fortune. As the senzall cleared, the man began to stir, so we hid to watch the fun.

I'd imagined he might jump about in surprise and pleasure, but this was not to be. Waking and rubbing his eyes, he believed himself to be dreaming still—this I could clearly read. Rising, he walked from room to room as if in a trance. Finally, he sat at the kitchen table and whispered, "Nice seeing you, Willa," and I could read the waves of regret and melancholy.

His emotion turned to something else as he slammed his fist on the table and said into the silence, "I won't let you down."

At first glance I saw the nostalgia and suspected a memory of Hazel. But it was himself he envisioned: a grinning boy who loved the

*forest, who loved to draw, and who loved
a girl named Willa. He determined that he
would not—could not—let that boy down ever
again.*

*At second glance, I saw the light of future
hope, and with determination glowing about
him, he collected his luggage, rolled his bed-
ding, packed his painting, and wrote a note,
which he fixed to the door. Then he clicked the
lock and drove away in the black auto ride
with loyal Eddie.*

*So determined was Vincent Meeker that I
could catch the brilliant edge of his willpower
far, far down the road.*

—R. Whistle Bright

CHAPTER 29

Years of Chances

I REREAD WHISTLE'S DESCRIPTION and thought about it all day long. Finally I decided to tell Mom the truth about Halloween night. I was certain that she would feel more compassion for a guy who was trying so hard, but I didn't get the reaction I'd hoped.

"I can't believe you went there by yourselves," she said gravely. "He could have been flipped out and paranoid—and there's no cell phone service on Wicket's Road, and Deb wasn't even at home! Honestly, Zell, I thought you had better judgment," she scolded, angry and worried.

I'd been kidding myself that Mom would warm to the idea of a reunion with my dad. Even as I heard myself speak, I had to admit that the whole encounter sounded pretty darn weird.

"But, Mom," I tried again, "he said he'd been sober for five years!"

"He can say anything he wants to, can't he?" Folding her arms like a shield, she rallied for the next argument.

"He seemed like a very nice guy," I added quietly.

"Then where has he been all these years?" she demanded. "Not a single phone call or letter. Not a word to let us know whether he was alive or . . ." She stopped and, for the briefest moment, looked as if she was in agony.

"He was afraid he'd be interrupting our happy lives!" I said, reciting his phrase exactly.

"Or we'd be interrupting his party," she returned, drawing her coolness around her. I was stunned at her flinty resentment, and I wondered if she carried it around all the time, packed away in one of her boxes.

"How did he look?" she finally asked.

"Well, he seemed healthy. He was a little messy, like I said—but that's only because he'd been working."

"Oh, it's just like the bad old days," she groaned.

"I think he's painting for a living. . . ." My words trailed off because I remembered I hadn't actually confirmed this detail.

Taking a deep breath, Mom closed her eyes, and when she opened them, she was composed.

"Look, honey, I know you want the happy ending," she said, with sympathy dripping from every word. "But sometimes the ending is just hard."

"If he was so bad, then why'd you get together in the first place?"

As she recalled those years, she smiled a fleeting smile. "We got together because we belonged together. But with his sad family and rotten genetics, he was a train wreck waiting to happen.

"His brother, Michael, died in a motorcycle accident when he was twenty-one. That's when Ed—his dad—started drinking again. Two years later, the poor old guy managed to drive off the North Plunkit Bridge into floodwater." Mom shivered. "At least he killed only himself.

"Vin just unraveled, and I realized that all my energy was being spent on saving a guy who couldn't be saved—not by me, anyhow."

"Mom, you're not being fair. That was then. Why don't you at least give him a chance?"

"Oh, Zelly." She sounded tired to the core. "I gave him years of chances."

Night fell uneasily over the loft, with Mom pretending to read a book in her bedroom while I wrestled with the strange events of the week. Staring out my window, I watched Plunkit's one traffic light turn red for nobody, and then I flopped into bed for a rotten sleep.

All night I dreamed of crying babies and angry grown-ups and slamming doors. When I finally woke in the morning, I was relieved to be out of that awful slumber and surprised to find Mom sitting at the foot of my bed.

The moment our eyes connected, she announced, "I'm going up to Wicket's Road to give that man a piece of my mind." Her face was puffy and tired-looking, as if she'd gotten a rotten night's sleep, too. "I don't know what he's up to," she muttered, "hanging around that empty house and painting by kerosene like some crazy van Gogh."

"Mom, I told you, he got permission from the daughter, who said he could stay there in return for some cleaning." I wanted to say more, but I couldn't exactly share what Whistle had written, that the house had magically mended itself and Vincent Meeker left with "determination glowing about him." Unless she suddenly regained her memories of Nutfolk Wood, I'd sound like a lunatic.

"Regardless"—Mom flipped her hand, dismissing my argument—"he's a bad influence, and I don't want you around him." She bobbed her head to cement her decision. "As long as we're in Plunkit," she ordered, "you stay away from that house."

CHAPTER 30

Stubborn Girls

"I'M KNOCKING!" WHISTLE'S voice was insistent, his little fist *tip-tap*ping on the top of my desk.

"Oh, hi, Whistle." I didn't bother to tell him that knocking was a request for entry, not an announcement of arrival.

"Did you hear any of that?" I asked. He'd appeared the moment Mom shut my bedroom door.

"Just the 'stay away from that house' part."

"She's really mad. She said my dad's a bad influence, and she's going up there to yell at him."

"Well, I didn't detect a bad influence, and any-how he won't be there," Whistle pointed out.

"What did he write on that note?" I asked.

"Stuff about business and money and dead-lines," he relayed, "and how happy he was to meet you."

"Whistle, are you sure he's a good guy? I mean, when I talked to Mom, she made him sound pretty messed up."

My internal compass was wavering with the two opposing views, both so certain and so final. I wasn't sure what to believe.

Whistle sat down on my dictionary and began swinging his legs. "He is as good as you," he said with an open expression.

Surprised at Whistle's appraisal, I asked, "Are you just saying that?"

"I don't just say things," he declared, insulted. "Whether I want to or not, I can feel the core of the person I read." His green eyes bored into me. "It doesn't matter how you appear, and it doesn't matter the words you choose or the colors you shine. I always know the truth."

"And the truth of my dad is good, right?"

"Right. And the truth of you is something more."

He gave me a funny look and then changed the subject.

"We had a lark at the house transformation," he said with a grin. "All the old toots got riled and wanted to work more on the project."

"I wish I could have seen it!" I said, imagining the magical renovation.

"They're going back," he added. "I think the job gave them energy and direction, you know?"

"Probably gives them hope," I agreed.

"And me, too," Whistle admitted with a faraway look.

I wished for Whistle's sake that his sketchy plans would somehow preserve Nutfolk Wood.

"Whistle, you should go before traffic picks up," I advised. "You could get stalled in a surge."

"I'm a careful fellow," he claimed. "Unusually skilled."

"Yes, and unusually boastful," I added.

With exaggerated shock, he tried to look offended. "Pesky rude of you to say so," he returned. Raising one eyebrow, he barely smiled and slowly surged away.

Mom returned from her fruitless trip up Wicket's Road. She placed my dad's note on the kitchen table where I sat eating a bowl of cereal.

"Well, the house looked good," she began. "But he's gone." With a mixture of irritation and something else—disappointment, I think—Mom slumped into the other kitchen chair and blew a noisy sigh. Pressing her fingers to her eyes, she said, "Go ahead, read the note."

Dear Zelly,

I am so happy to have met you. A million things are running through my mind right now, but first on the list is money. I am leaving to get some things in order, and I hope to return when I complete my deadlines and rearrange some business.

Best Regards,
V. Meeker

"Zelly." Mom was solemn. "This stuff about deadlines and business . . . He's just not . . . trustworthy." Her jaw tightened, and her face hardened into the picture of a stubborn woman.

"I won't have you jerked around like this," she warned. "I won't have it."

But I was stubborn, too. I wanted to see my dad again, to feel that connection, to mend that gap. For the first time ever, I felt secure in my place in the world, and I knew it was from being in Plunkit, from my friendships with Lupine and Frederick and Whistle. And from finding my dad.

I did not intend to lose him again.

Thinking her own troublesome thoughts, Mom

pursed her lips and frowned, but if she had been paying attention, she would have seen the same clenched jaw on a girl who was just as stubborn as she was.

CHAPTER 31

Transformations

"SOMETHING WEIRD IS going on."

It was Lupine again, trying to sound all dramatic on the phone.

"There's always something weird going on with you," I pointed out.

"This is serious!" she exclaimed. "Jimi Hart is nailing a SOLD notice on the Wickets' FOR SALE sign."

"Run out and ask him who bought it!" I cried.

"Okay, I'll bring the phone." Immediately, rustling and foot-pounding ensued.

"Mr. Hart?" I could hear Lupine's high-pitched voice. "Who bought this property?" she sweetly asked.

"Beat it, kid" was the grumpy retort.

"Come on, we're the closest neighbors. You may as well tell me," Lupine coaxed.

"I said, get lost."

"How rude!" Lupine admonished. Then, rustle, rustle. "Hello, Zelly? Someone just drove up. It's a Glen Wood truck! Hold on. I think I'll just hang around for a minute." More annoying shuffling sounds made me think she was putting the phone in her pocket.

A car door slammed, and a man bellowed, "Hart! I thought we talked about a deal?"

"Yeah, Lou, we talked, but some guy beat you to the punch. Flew to Palm Springs and buttered up the old lady."

"Did he make a better offer?"

"Nope. Got it for a song."

"Who is this guy?"

"Some tree hugger. He promised he'd never develop since that's what dear departed Granny would have wanted."

"Are you serious?"

"Yeah, I'm serious. And it seriously reduced my percentage," Hart complained. Suddenly angry again, he shouted, "Hey! I told you to get lost."

Lupine's nervous giggle accompanied more muffled thumps that sounded like jogging. Then *bump bump bump*, up the stairs, and *bang!* That must have been the trailer door.

"What a jerk," I heard her say to herself. Then, "Hello, Zelly?" She was loud and clear now. "It sounds like the right person bought that property!"

I had to respect how Lupine stood up to cranky Mr. Hart, even after he told her to get lost. "Lupine, you've got some nerve."

"That's what my mom always says."

Weeks passed without one word from Vincent Meeker, which made me worry despite Whistle's assertion that he was a good guy. Was it possible that the "determined glow" that Whistle described was my dad's resolve to get the heck out of Plunkit?

Aunt Viv went ahead and had her knee surgery, so Mom was busier than ever at the store—although she left no doubt that we were leaving before Christmas. Still furious about how I had snuck up to Hazel's and met my dad, Mom had not wavered in her opinion of him. I'd been grounded and working in the store after school, until Mom finally relented and let me return to Lupine's, but only after Deb relayed that Jimi Hart had installed a metal gate at the entrance of the Wickets' driveway, and no one had gone in or out since the day that he had locked it.

November crept to its end, and the usual stormy showers doused the last of autumn's color. The landscape was pretty in a wintry way, with bare branches, windswept fields, and that wide-open sky.

When the bus dropped us off at the hairpin, we were blasted with a startling gust of wind that sent

Frederick's loose paperwork flying. Laughing, we ran around trying to catch it all.

"We've only got an hour before my mom gets home," Lupine complained. "Frederick, you should have packed your homework properly," she scolded, grabbing at two more of his papers.

"I need a secretary," he moaned, stooping for his math worksheet, now defaced by his big footprint.

"Be your own secretary," Lupine mumbled, true to form.

We dropped our backpacks at the door of the Gypsy Wagon and wasted no time in hiking to the homestead.

From the knoll, we could see that the house had been painted bright yellow, with black shutters framing the windows. We reached the front yard and appraised more changes, noting that the chimney had been restored with pretty rocks from the stream, and the shingles on the roof looked like newly split shakes. The old maple now stretched its limbs over a trim, green lawn, and all the outbuildings had been repaired and reroofed and now were barn red, like proper country sheds.

"Wow!" Frederick exclaimed. "Did the Nutfolk do all of this?"

"They must have," Lupine insisted. "That gate has stayed locked, and there's no sign of tire tracks. Plus, I haven't heard a hammer bang or a human voice coming from this place. I mean, how can you reroof a house without making a sound?"

Walking around the property, we admired the cute outbuildings, the pruned apple trees, and the weeded garden beds. Even though the house was locked up and the ladder was gone, we could peek in the porch windows and ooh and ahh at the cozy interior.

It was all so pretty that I wished my mom could see it. I bet it was nicer than when she was a kid.

"Whoever bought it sure got a cute place," I

said. "And hopefully, Nutfolk Wood will be safe."

"Come on," Lupine urged, checking her watch. "We've got less than forty minutes to visit Whistle and get back to my house."

We found the town in a whirlwind of activity. Little people were everywhere, washing windows, sweeping porches, fixing chimneys, and patching roofs. The LEAVE BE sign had been removed from the jamb of the stump house, and cheerful lights lit the house from within. When Whistle stepped onto the porch with some bread and jam, I was surprised.

"What are you doing in the stump house?" I asked.

"Before she was a Bright, my momby was a Nutbone," he explained, "which makes this our rightful home. It was just that after my parents died, Auntie didn't care for the stump. Too big and drafty, she used to say. But now we've got folks surging in who need lodging."

"Why all the company?" I asked, marveling at

the shimmering Nutfolk cleaning and repairing the shabby town.

"They've come for the project," Whistle said between big bites of bread.

"You mean Hazel's house?"

He nodded and gulped.

"But it's all done and sold," I pointed out.

"It's the home-sweet-home factor," Whistle replied. "The final touches. Plus, if all goes well, townsfolk plan to return."

Grampy joined him on the porch with a thimble-sized mug of something hot. He was smug when he said, "It was worth the sweat to catch a good hum. Now we just want to keep 'm caught."

"Do you know who bought the house?" I asked, suddenly nervous about hearing the answer.

"Our Whistle tells us that the glow on that question is good," Grampy said with confidence.

"So, who is it, Whistle?"

"That I can't tell you specifically." He shrugged.

"But I caught impressions from Mr. Hart that were favorable."

"A fair hum has taken claim," Grampy summed up, "and that's the main thing."

"Yes, I guess so."

Surrounded by the Nutfolk commotion, I suddenly realized how unnecessary it all was.

"Why are you doing this work by hand?" I asked. "Why don't you just do your surgey thing?"

"It's good, honest work," Grampy declared, "and we'd grow fat and silly indeed if we always took the easy path."

A noisy spit was his exclamation point, and he repeated the words with a smile because he liked the sound of them so well. "Fat and silly indeed."

CHAPTER 32

Regular Life

CHRISTMAS WAS A week away, and now that school was out for the holiday, Mom insisted I start packing to return to the city. It was like one of those dreams where you're trying to get away, like you're trying to climb out of quicksand but never make any progress. I was trying to stay in Plunkit, and no matter what I said or did, I couldn't get anywhere with my mom.

Deb had invited us to her Christmas Day brunch, but Mom was being so stubborn, she wouldn't even consider it. "We'll be back in the city on Christmas Day," she'd stated, as if the stupid plan couldn't be changed. I argued, finagled, and begged. I did everything except cry, but she simply would not budge.

When a large box was delivered to the bookstore, I read the return address and felt a thrill. It was from him. Finally! Maybe he could convince my mom to stay.

Eyeing the package, Mom frowned and made a growling sound of disapproval. It wasn't until after closing the store that she would even look at the box, and then she felt the need to make a little speech before unwrapping it. "Zelly, I want it understood that we are moving back to the city. I'm going back to teaching, and you are going back to the University International School."

"But I don't want to go back," I objected for the hundredth time. "I'm doing rotten there, and I don't fit in!"

"You're not doing that badly," Mom chided, ripping a long strip of tape off the side.

"But I like it here, and I like the kids here."

"Honey, I've tried to make it clear all along that the past is staying in the past." Mom's cheeks burned with emotion, but her tone was unyielding.

"What about the store?" I argued. "What if Aunt Viv wants to retire?"

"Then I'll hire a manager. Or I'll sell. Either way, we are returning to our regular lives."

"Why can't this be our regular life?" I yelled.

Mom was ripping the last strip of tape when the sides flipped open and packing peanuts spilled to the floor. He'd sent her a painting.

In the middle of an exquisite spring landscape sat the familiar stump, only in this version there were no doors or windows, no surrounding cabins, and no central park or shopping center. In fact, there were no little people at all. It was a glen without Nutfolk.

"*Nature's Magic*," Mom said, reading the title at the edge. "His mother painted it. It used to hang in Hazel's living room, and she said it was the one thing she'd run back for if the house was on fire."

I remembered the rectangle of white on the wall

and figured he must have snuck it out of Hazel's house to restore it.

"Is there a note?" I asked.

Mom rummaged through the debris and found an envelope labeled *Willa*.

"I'd like to read this alone," she said curtly.

"Fine." Torn between curiosity and heartbreak, I stalked off and ran up the stairs.

Banging around in the kitchen, I intended to make spaghetti, but as I filled a pot with water, I realized the need to wipe tears off my face. Funny how crying snuck up on me like that. No great tragedy occurred, just a fight with my mom. I coughed out a couple of sobs, foreign-sounding and strange in my ears, and then I had myself a little cry.

I had to admit that I felt better, not so angry and frustrated. And nothing bad happened. Nothing horrible transpired because of it. That little voice had been wrong.

Setting the pot aside, I splashed water on my face and blew my nose. I tiptoed back downstairs and found Mom sitting on the floor behind the counter. Except for the lit window display and the cold glow from the outside streetlamp, the room was dark.

"What'd he say?" I asked quietly.

With a grimace she handed me the note. Holding it up to the window light, I read:

Dear Wil,

Now that I am clean and sober, I would like to apologize for so many things. We could go for a walk on Wicket's Road and clear the air between us. It's presumptuous, I know, but I thought on Christmas Day the store would be closed, and you'd have the time off, and we could meet then. I hope you'll bring Zelly if she'd like to come.

Wil, if it seems like too much water has passed under this bridge, it's okay to just let it go.

V.

"Seems sort of nice" was my opinion.

Mom frowned harder. "It's one of those letters," she sneered, saying "letters" as if it were a dirty word. "He needs to be forgiven so he can move on."

I wanted to blurt out that he was thinking of her more than himself and that he was just being careful and respectful, but I realized it was my blind intuition, and I couldn't be a hundred percent sure.

"Why Christmas?" she snapped. "Like I don't have a life or a family of my own? Like I don't have anything better to do on Christmas Day than chase after him?" Shaking her head, she heaved a gloomy sigh. "Typical self-absorbed behavior. Just like the bad old days."

CHAPTER 33

Wintertell

I OPENED MY WINDOW and looked out on the street. In the clean, frozen atmosphere the stars were prickly points of light, and the air delivered the kind of cold that's a shock to eyeballs and lungs. In the intersection, the stoplight switched to green, but no cars passed, no people stirred. Saving the melancholy scene in my mind, I shivered and closed the window, and then even under five lofty blankets, it was a long while before I was warm.

At first, my dream world was as icy as the real one, when for no particular reason, I found myself transported to the woods, walking barefoot toward the Secret Garden.

My toes were freezing and tingly, and I regretted not bringing slippers or throwing on a bathrobe over my old white nightie. But as I wandered farther into the woods, I began to grow warm. In a dream bubble that defied the weather, I felt safe in body and mind.

The path was unusually smooth and clear, with marker leaves glowing to show the way. More leaves blinked on, and more, until thousands glowed to light the path all the way to Nutfolk Wood. Far above, the stars glittered, and all around, leaves twinkled like Christmas lights in the night. From the glen drifted music, where strings and flutes and small voices combined in strange and haunting song.

I stepped into the clearing and saw the whole population gathered in the green, dining at tables covered in white linen. The surrounding dwellings looked charming and clean, with fresh paint and new shingles, as pretty as Hazel's old house.

Lighting the park were countless globes on sticks, reflecting off the white linen, the polished silverware, and the gleaming candleholders. Instead of their customary brown and green tunics, the Nutfolk wore colorful dresses and vests with bright stockings and funny boots. Like exotic birds, they were splashes of vivid color, out of place in the cold evergreen wood.

I spotted Whistle and smiled to see him in a yellow waistcoat, which at first seemed hilarious compared to his old brown shirt—like seeing Huck Finn in a dinner jacket. But I had to admit he was handsome in yellow. I had to admit he was handsome!

Feeling suddenly huge and self-conscious, I wished I could be little like everyone else, and with the wish, it was so. A tiny Zelly crept toward the tables but stayed in the shadows.

Auntie Win stepped up to the gazebo and introduced herself to the crowd. "As your healer and the first teller of tales, I best get things moving or we'll be here all night."

The audience chuckled and rapped spoons on the tables to show their approval.

"I know a boy," she began, "who came from the finest folk, whose beginnings were uneasy. In the winter of terrible cold, he was but two springs, and even then he was precocious. In him we saw the mood catcher, to be sure. Quiet he was, and watchful, and always one step ahead of his tired-out poppy."

The crowd snickered.

Detecting a wild expression in Whistle's eyes, I realized he felt trapped. He wasn't the sort of boy who enjoyed the spotlight, but he had to endure it. It was the kind of spectacle that kids have to suffer through for the sake of their elders.

"I remember the fateful night," his aunt recounted. "Cold enough to freeze your spit before it touched the ground, when traders arrived from Forkton, telling of a crash down the hum town road. Bad it was, with two vehicles and four humans in distress. The traders said there were no doctors coming, because no one saw the sight but Nutfolk, and the vehicles lay steaming and hidden in the ditch.

"My younger sister, Stillness, was the healer then. She left hurriedly on a mercy trip with her good man, Ralph Bright. They rode the jay ship, cautiously as they were surging on the main road.

"Stillness checked the injured that night, healing where she could and administering bandages and the like. Then, to attract attention, she and Ralph surged branches to burn in the road, which was when the terrible truck sped through. Before they died, our loved ones lit the flame to ensure that help would arrive for those humans still trapped in the ditch."

Here, Auntie Win paused to sweep a pinkie to her heart, as did everyone else in the crowd.

"So their boy became my boy," she said, "and I was so lucky to have him." She smiled at Whistle with dewy eyes, while he tried his best to sit up and look dignified.

"Twelve springs have passed since that dreadful night, and our boy has grown up clever and strong. The best mood catcher since . . . well, since me." Her wry smile made the audience laugh. "But always there was a burning angst, and I feared the boy's anger would take its toll. A loathing of humans tainted his youth, until he crossed paths with the real thing.

"Human children, he discovered, were not so different from himself, and each day it became harder and harder to keep up his old habit of hate. One noon on passing, I gave the boy a quick read, and to my shock, the familiar burn was gone. Completely gone! In its place glowed the pleasant hue of fun.

"I told myself long ago that if Ronald Whistle Bright could douse that fire, I'd toast him at Wintertell for all to applaud."

Turning toward Whistle, she raised a glass that

appeared in her hand and toasted. "Here, here, Mr. Bright!"

"Here, here!" the audience called as one, their spoons tapping and their voices echoing joyfully through the silent, frozen wood.

Reluctantly, Whistle stood, his face betraying a funny combination of embarrassment and pride. I was startled when he turned my way and, smiling, toasted me . . . or so it seemed.

As another storyteller took the podium, Whistle vanished from his chair, and he was suddenly standing next to me. Now that we were the same size, his familiar glow took me by surprise. Like a walking ember, he radiated a golden, flickering light as well as a tangible warmth. In his silly yellow coat, he was all brightness and heat.

"Hey, Whistle," I said. "Am I dreaming?"

"Sort of" was his vague answer.

"We're leaving Plunkit tomorrow," I whispered, "but thanks for the dream. It's beautiful, and I'll remember it always—if you don't fog my brain for security."

I smirked, and so did he.

"You'll remember it," he said assuredly.

I nodded and glanced down at my nightgown, suddenly self-conscious. "Can you get me home?"

"You are home," he said, and leaning forward, he kissed me on the lips.

I woke with a jolt, the electric charge still moving from my lips to my fingertips and down to my toes.

In the darkness of my bedroom, all I could say was "Wow!"

Chapter 34

Relief

"**A**RE YOU STILL teaching brats at that fancy school of yours?" G.G. had always disapproved of the exclusive Smarty Pants U.

"I've been on a leave of absence. I told you, Grandma," Mom tiredly explained. "I've been working at the bookstore and sorting Mama's stuff."

After being in the city for two days, Mom insisted we visit G.G. at the Laurel Arms. This was the last thing in the world I wanted to do, because G.G. was always a grouch and Mom and I were barely speaking. But Mom said it was our duty since it was Christmas Eve and no other relatives could stand my great-grandmother.

We found her sitting in the lounge with her usual gang of old lady friends watching *It's a Wonderful Life*.

Mom presented her with a fuzzy sweater, and I gave her a little landscape I'd painted. As if on cue, her gang oohed and ahhed vigorously, which for G.G. was even better than the gifts themselves. Then we rolled G.G.'s wheelchair to a more private corner, where she felt free to dispense with the niceties and get down to criticizing.

"The store is where you ought to be," she grumbled, "not teaching a bunch of eggheads who don't appreciate our Hazel Jo."

You could have knocked me over with a feather to hear G.G. stick up for me like that!

Doing a double take, Mom exclaimed, "I'm surprised to hear you say that, Grandma. I know that you don't approve of the International School, but I didn't realize you liked Plunkit so much. After all, it's so full of 'trashy hippies' and 'down-and-out loggers.'"

"Well, it's not so trashy anymore." G.G. sniffed. Then, tilting her head, she studied Mom with her one good eye. "Willa, you've gained weight," she decreed.

Although this remark may have distressed some women, Mom had been bugged all her life about being too skinny, so she knew that G.G. was actually giving her a compliment.

"Whatever you're doing," G.G. advised, "do it some more."

Her grandmother's sideways praise, as well as the perceptive comment about me, left Mom visibly shaken—hearing compliments coming from G.G. was like watching a dog talk.

"We've got to go!" Mom said abruptly. Grabbing my hand, she dragged me through the lobby and toward the door as fast as she could. "Merry Christmas, Grandma," she called out over her shoulder. "We'll see you soon!"

Back in the car, we drove south on Highway

99, across town toward the apartment. As the windshield wipers swatted at fat drops of sleet, we passed block after block of strip malls. Night fell, and streetlights blinked on, illuminating the concrete landscape. Compared to the gentle countryside of Plunkit, the endless wires and poles and cement looked like a sci-fi nightmare. Everything felt hard-edged and dismally cold.

Whistle could never visit me here. It was way too dangerous with all the cars and technology. Plus, he'd hate it anyway, just like I did.

Peeking at Mom through my eyelashes, I realized G.G. was right: Mom had gained weight. In fact, she had more color and sparkle than I could ever remember, but the city seemed to paralyze her. She didn't want to unpack. She didn't want to call her principal. She didn't want to get groceries. She didn't want to be here! So what were we doing?

Suddenly, I lunged forward and my head almost hit the dashboard as Mom slammed on the brakes at a red light.

"Sorry," she winced, embarrassed. "I wasn't paying attention." We were moving again when she said, "I'm going to stop in here for a cup of coffee," and pulled into a mini-mart. "You want anything?"

"I'll look around," I said, distant and cool. We were still acting stiff with each other, mostly because we hadn't resolved anything. She was absolutely determined to protect me from my "loser" dad, and I was determined to get to know him. Plus, she never regained the slightest memory of Nutfolk Wood, and it was all that I could think about.

I followed Mom into the mini-mart and squinted in the glare of the fluorescent lights that buzzed along with the bad Christmas music. I was about to check the candy aisle when something else caught my eye.

On the magazine rack, a picture swept me back to Halloween night: a moody, fall image of dead leaves swirling in a darkened sky. I was looking at the cover art for a news magazine, and although the headline announced an uneasy stock market, I recognized the image at once.

My heart racing, I stepped closer to examine the picture. This could prove that my dad had told the truth when he wrote about completing deadlines— like a conscientious guy, not like a loser.

I grabbed the magazine and, checking the byline, discovered that the artist wasn't named Meeker. Instead it said, *Cover art by Vinyn Wil.*

For a short moment my brain stalled over the unfamiliar name, but as I made the connection, my eyes bugged out. *Vin and Wil forever.* He'd chosen that declaration for his pseudonym. It was so corny, and sad, and romantic.

Hugging the magazine, I knew that Mom would listen to him now. "Mom!" I shouted. "I want to get this."

In the parking lot of the mini-mart, Mom and I sat in the car with the heater going. She flipped to the byline in the magazine and stared.

"It's him," I said again. "I saw him working on the painting at Hazel's house."

Shaking her head in quiet disbelief, Mom's face traveled through four different emotions: confusion, doubt, comprehension, and last, a guarded delight.

We returned to our apartment on Forty-fifth Street. Our luggage was still sitting in the living room, where we'd dumped it two days ago. Although we'd gotten out the toothbrushes, everything else remained packed. Our luggage, our apartment, me, Mom: everything was the same, yet everything felt different. There was an excitement whirling around us like the itchy wind that Whistle had created to push me up the trail.

Timidly Mom asked, "So, what did he say about Christmas Day?"

"He said to meet on Wicket's Road." I remembered the note word for word.

Mom nodded. "Do you want to go on this weird rendezvous?"

"Definitely."

"Then let's go," she said. "Let's go right now!" Grinning, she grabbed me in a bear hug and whispered in my ear, "Thanks, Zel."

CHAPTER 35

Weird Rendezvous

ALIGHT SNOW HAD dusted Plunkit, giving the old town a new, clean look. Since the heat in the loft had been turned off, we ended up sleeping together in Mom's room, glad for each other's company and the warmth. By midmorning, we were eating breakfast and celebrating our own little Christmas.

I gave Mom a book of maps and a heart necklace purchased with money I'd earned when I was grounded and working at the bookstore. She gave me a stand-up easel and oil paints and two canvases. But I couldn't help thinking that, this year, Christmas wasn't so much about the stuff.

I dressed hurriedly for the weather, while Mom spent an hour deciding what to wear. She primped in the mirror for another hour, which wasn't like her. Finally, stepping out in her cream-colored wool coat and a cashmere beret, she looked very put together and as pretty as I'd ever seen her.

"How do I look?" she nervously asked.

"Like G.G. said, whatever you're doing, keep doing it," I said, smiling.

After carefully negotiating Wicket's Road, Mom parked in front of the Gypsy Wagon in almost four inches of snow. Marla's car was there, as were those of several others who'd come for Deb's Christmas brunch.

Deb appeared on the front porch and called out, "What's going on?" Marla soon joined her and waved while Lupine and Frederick grinned from the windows.

"It's a rendezvous!" Mom called back. "But don't get your hopes up, girls." She gave her old friends a knowing look. Apparently, no further explanation was needed.

"Hope's a good thing!" Marla returned.

Staring ahead, Mom and I stood at the open gate, the fresh tire tracks in the snow pointing the way.

"He must have gone back to Hazel's old place," Mom said with a worried expression.

I just kept my mouth shut and started walking.

Under our boots, the snow crunched with that squeaky, cold sound that only snow makes. The field was quilted in a layer of white, and the Doug firs stood like flocked Christmas trees, majestic and soaring.

I noticed Mom's pink cheeks and glassy eyes, and her lips moving in pretend conversation. Perhaps plotting out what she would say to my dad. Smirking, I wondered how I would explain what had happened here. *Um, fairies fixed your house, Mr. Meeker.* Yeah, right.

Mom's private dialogue ceased when we reached

the yellow house, as fresh and startling now as a sunflower in the snow.

"I can imagine Hazel peeking out the screen door and calling me to come eat my lunch," she said, full of emotion.

The tire tracks ended where the black truck was parked under the rebuilt carport. From there came a steady line of footprints crossing the yard to the porch, where a plain wreath had been hung and a doormat spelled out WELCOME, FRIENDS.

Inside the house glowed a warm, yellow light, a happy contrast to the cold, white surroundings. With the bright-eyed windows and smoke curling from the chimney, the house looked like a child's drawing of home.

"It's weird how good this place looks," Mom observed. "It never looked this good, even when Hazel was alive—and I don't remember those shutters," she mumbled, her lips scrunched in puzzlement. "Vin went all out." Her words trickled away, and she seemed unable to move forward, so

I reached out and took her hand, and we stepped up on the porch.

Mom rapped on the door and then just stared straight ahead. Out of the corner of my eye, I spotted the balloon and jay-ship approaching from the north woods. The bird was refreshed with a coat of new paint, and apparently Grampy had finished his carving because the silhouette revealed a sharp beak and crest. I hoped the Nutfolk didn't intend to start chucking acorns again, because those heavy suckers could do some damage!

Just as before, the knock on the door triggered a clatter of a dog's nails on wood, and after a noisy round of barking and shushing, Vincent Meeker opened the door wide.

CHAPTER 36

Shiny and Happy

"COME IN, COME in!"

Wildly happy and awkward at the same time, he ushered us into the hall. His cheeks were blushing scarlet, and his teeth seemed very white against the color. Startled again by the familiarity of his features, I felt as if I were looking at the boy version of me.

He'd trimmed his hair and shaved his scraggly beard, revealing the lines and scars of harder times. Still, his was a pleasing face with depth and character, ready to smile, able to cry.

While Eddie sniffed and wagged and slobbered, we stood uneasily in the front hall, until Mr.

Meeker said haltingly, "I must admit I'm a little confused."

"About what?" Mom asked.

"This house seems to have gone on without me," he replied helplessly.

"Vin, are you . . . okay?" Mom started to look disappointed.

Racing to say something plausible that might explain the crazy situation, I blustered, "He's fine! It's just . . . he's surprised because the estate has been fixing the house."

With a grateful glance my way, he said, "That's right, the estate!"

"I don't understand," Mom interjected.

By the look on his face, he didn't understand either, only he didn't want to admit it and sound like an idiot. Instead, he fell back on, "Let's sit in the parlor and talk."

The subdued light of the kerosene and the tint from the fire in the woodstove gave the room a copper glow. With the painted tan walls, gleaming wood floor, and the new rock hearth, everything seemed clean and rich.

In observance of the holiday, evergreen garlands topped all the windows, giving the space a piney fragrance. In one corner, a little Christmas tree sprouted from a rustic log. Its decor of red berries and ropes of pale moss looked suspiciously Nutfolk in style, but what was really distracting was the golden acorn that hovered in midair over the top of the small tree.

I checked the eyes of my mom and Mr. Meeker. They weren't seeing the acorn, but the sight of the floating ornament left me rattled. Fidgeting, I continued to stand while Mom went and sat on the sofa.

"I understand you've been working on your art," Mom began. She seemed composed, but I knew better by the way she was strangling her gloves.

"Business is good," he returned, his neck and ears flushing hot pink.

Oh, this was painful. They seemed to be horribly

uncomfortable, but at the same time all shiny and happy. In fact, I would have sworn that their happiness shimmered around them, but it was only a trick of light from the setting sun.

Outside the window, the stupid jay-ship arrived with Grampy and Whistle on board. They were waving and pointing at the floating acorn, which still hovered several inches above the Christmas tree. What the heck did they want me to do?

CHAPTER 37

Honorable

MY EYES PRACTICALLY crossed, I was so distracted by sensory overload: the floating acorn, Grampy and Whistle waving from the jay-ship, my dad's ears red enough to melt . . .

"Excuse me!" I blurted. "I think I'll just step outside for a minute."

On the porch, it was soothing and cold. Taking a deep breath, I exhaled and hissed, "What are you guys doing?"

"Come to collect our gold!" Grampy barked, surprised as always by how dense we humans could be. "Got it waiting above that gee-gawed tree so's we could find it."

"Coincidence, eh?" Whistle added. "I mean, that we chose your poppy on the day of the funeral."

"Chose him for what?" I tried to keep my voice down.

"Our good deed."

"I don't understand."

"We dropped one acorn to mark your gramby's passing," he said slowly, as if I were simpleminded. "And we planted another one as our good deed."

"But where did you plant it?"

"In your poppy's coat pocket."

"Did he know?"

"Course not!"

"Does the acorn have some kind of power?"

"It's a lump of gold," Whistle drawled. "How could it have any power?"

Recalling the day he tapped Lupine and Frederick on their ankles for a clearer view, I realized that Whistle Bright was the one with all the power.

"Then why'd you plant it?" I asked, utterly frustrated.

"Tradition!" Whistle replied, impatient with

explanations that were so elementary and obvious, to Nutfolk anyway.

"The deed isn't to give a gift of gold." Whistle
laughed. "'Twas the flash of insight your poppy
gained. Clarity, to make good choices."

The boy vanished but soon returned with the
heavy acorn, which tilted the jay-ship when it
was loaded. Whistle and Grampy began drifting
north, their sights set for Nutfolk Wood.

Following them across the yard to the carport,
I called out, "Whistle, wait!" with my arm outstretched.

He and the acorn surged onto my palm as my
hair rose and crackled with the static.

"I'm right here," he said evenly.

Tingling with the charge of the senzall so close,
I whispered, "Was Wintertell a dream or was it
real?"

His green eyes locked into mine. "It was almost
real."

Determined, I tried to clarify the thing that
bothered me most: that kiss. "What about when

you toasted me? And the *other thing*? What was that all about?"

With a decidedly wicked smile, he said, "That was my dream."

"What's that supposed to mean?"

"When I figure it out, you'll be the first to know." Grinning, he began to disappear with the noisy feedback that accompanied a hectic surge. Through the static he added, "The acorn is yours for now. Zelly, the Nutfolk thank you, and so do I."

With a final, squeaky buzz, he was gone, leaving me holding the acorn.

I squeezed my fingers around the gold, my hand still tingling from the senzall. And that's when I saw it. Beneath the trinket in the middle of my palm was the telltale mark: *For aid and protection of the folk and their property.* Just like my mother, I was an Honorable, and I had the acorn tattoo to prove it.

I'm Good

As I watched the balloon disappear into the woods, I noticed it was snowing again. In the blue twilight, the falling snow gave the yard, the field, and the woods beyond an isolated, muffled feel, as hushed and breathless as when a good song ends.

I slipped back into the hall and quietly shut the door behind me, pausing to listen to the adults for just a moment. Softly, earnestly, my dad was saying, "I couldn't call until I proved it to myself."

"I thought the worst," she said.

"For a while it was bad," he admitted. "For a while I was . . . Wil, I'm glad you made me leave—for your sake as well as for hers. You always were a very wise girl."

"Vin, what now?" she asked, as I had.

He was quiet for a bit and sounded timid when he finally answered. "I have a new studio. Maybe you would like to come for dinner sometime."

Mom's tone was doubtful. "Where is this new studio?" she asked.

"Right here—this house."

"You bought this house?"

"Yeah, I did."

Peeking around the corner, I saw that Mr. Meeker was smiling sheepishly at Mom, while her expression was one of amazement. He was still sitting on the chair by the window, she on the opposite couch, but they were leaning in toward each other, as if the space between them was magnetic. They both turned when I entered, and in unison said, "Zelly, are you okay?"

Stepping into the golden parlor, I glanced out the window, where the snow was falling harder.

But inside this rebuilt house, it was warm, with a fire in the stove and that sparkle in my parents' eyes. Their attention was all mine now, and their smiles included me in the cozy picture.

"I'm good," I answered, and I meant it.

Maybe Whistle gave me some insight that day, or perhaps it was my own intuition, but a little voice in my head told me that Mom would not take me from Plunkit. Not now. There was too much to hope for here.

When I see that girl, she looks like sunrise and springtime. And she feels like goodness and fun. Shiny as a mood catcher, she seems hardly human in her glow . . . that girl called Zelly, just like a fairy.

—R. Whistle Bright